What She Wants at Midnight

What She Wants
at Midnight

KIMBERLY DEAN

POCKET BOOKS

New York   London   Toronto   Sydney

Pocket Books
A Division of Simon & Schuster, Inc.
1230 Avenue of the Americas
New York, NY 10020

First Pocket Books trade paperback edition March 2008

POCKET and colophon are registered trademarks of Simon & Schuster, Inc.

For information about special discounts for bulk purchases, please contact Simon & Schuster Special Sales at 1-800-456-6798 or business@simonandschuster.com.

Manufactured in the United States of America

10 9 8 7 6 5 4 3 2 1

Library of Congress Cataloging-in-Publication Data
Dean, Kimberly.
   What she wants at midnight / Kimberly Dean.—1st Pocket
Books trade pbk. ed.
        p. cm.
ISBN-13: 978-1-4165-4745-7
ISBN-10:   1-4165-4745-2
PS3604.E152W47 2008
813'.6—dc22
                                          2007048958

To my agent, Jessica

Thanks

Prologue

H e watched her while she slept.

His eyes were haunting, nearly the color of midnight. Eyes full of lust. Eyes full of need.

He came to her every night, but she didn't know his name. She'd never seen his face.

Only his eyes.

Tonight they looked down on her with a desire so intense, it made her writhe on the crisp white sheets of her bed. Heat poured through her veins. She wanted him so badly. In vain, she kicked off the covers, trying to ease her distress.

His eyes sparked, and his blistering gaze ran down her form. Yet he did not touch.

He *never* touched. He only watched.

She slid to the side of the bed, trying to get closer to where he stood over her. Her nightgown rode high on her thighs and dipped low between her aching breasts.

She wanted to see him. Wanted to know his face. His body.

She desperately *needed* to know his body.

Fighting through the weight of the fog, she lifted her hand toward him. Just once, she needed to touch him.

His eyelids drooped and, for a moment, she thought he'd let her. Her fingers brushed whisper-close to his brow, but he retreated. Regret made the luminous light of his eyes dim.

"No," she whispered, instinctively knowing what was to come. "Stay with me."

Tormented, his dark eyes closed.

Then he was gone.

Devon came awake with a jolt, her body throbbing. With a groan, she collapsed back onto the mattress.

When was she going to stop doing this to herself? When would she learn?

Her dream man was only that.

A dream.

One

"I can't believe you're still dreaming about him."

Devon glanced up from the stargazer lilies she was contemplating and caught her friend's concerned look. At once, she regretted mentioning her nighttime flight of fancy. "I can't either, but I don't have any control over my thoughts when I sleep."

"Of course you do. It's *your* mind. Next time it happens, tell your little dream self to jump his bones." Tasha gestured with both hands for emphasis. "For heaven's sake, you two should be on your third pass through the Kama Sutra by now."

Devon blushed and moved farther down the aisle of the greenhouse. It was late, nearly closing time, and the cavernous Quonset hut made their voices carry.

"It's not like that," she said in a hushed tone. "We don't touch . . . we can't. He just watches."

Tasha groaned. "Honey, what are you doing in that bed?"

"I don't . . . I haven't . . . He just makes me hot, all right?" Devon tucked her hair behind her ear, uncomfortable talking about something so private but knowing there was no use trying to hide it. Tasha knew her better than anyone, and she'd never been able to keep anything from her. "This has been going on for seven months. It's making me crazy."

"It's making me worried. This isn't natural, Dev."

But it felt natural. Instinctive. *Right.*

Devon stared hard at the 'Shadeglow' impatiens in their little plastic seedling containers. The dream overtaking her life was unlike any she'd ever had before—and not only because it wouldn't go away. Every time she slipped under, she was caught in a world so vivid and tactile, her senses sang. And when she awoke, she remembered everything in such detail, she'd swear it had been real.

Her body certainly couldn't tell the difference. She tended to slip so seamlessly from sleep to wakefulness, the two blended together. The resulting sexual frustration was driving her insane. If she woke one more time to find her skin sweaty, her heart pounding, and dampness coating her thighs . . .

A familiar tightness sizzled low in her belly, and she determinedly pushed it away.

"I've checked out all the dream interpretation books at the library," she confessed. "Dreams about eyes supposedly signify enlightenment or understanding. The way this one is recurring, though, means that I'm not confronting something."

"Well, we both know what *that* is."

Devon glanced up sharply. "We do?"

"You need to confront the fact that it's time you got laid!"

Devon glanced around quickly. The greenhouse where they were shopping was on the outskirts of Solstice. Business was slow, and there were only a few other people around, but she didn't need them hearing about her sex life—or lack thereof. "Is that all you ever think about?" she hissed.

"It's been a three-month dry spell for me, too. I can't help it if I have sex on the brain." Tasha's chin lifted and a familiar stubborn look settled on her face. "Besides, that's why we're here."

Oh, really?

Devon got uneasy when her friend started digging into her purse. She should have known something was up. She loved gardening, but Tasha wasn't the kind of woman who planted flowers. She received them in bouquets from men.

"Aha! Here it is." Triumphantly, Tasha produced a folded piece of paper. She opened it with a flick of her wrist.

"What is that?" Devon asked apprehensively.

"Before you is the answer to all our problems."

"Why do I get the feeling I'm not going to like this?"

"Because you probably won't. That's why I didn't tell you earlier." Tasha smoothed the piece of paper almost reverently. "We're going to perform a love spell."

Before Devon could think of a thing to say, Tasha was picking up a red basket and determinedly moving toward the herbs section.

"Wait a minute!" Devon hurried to catch up, her long legs quickly matching her friend's shorter stride.

"We're going to perform it tonight," Tasha said in a tone that brooked no argument. "So you can stop worrying about those pesky, unsatisfying dreams. Before long, a real man will be warming your bed."

Devon fought for her patience. "Where did you get that?"

"The Internet." Tasha's stiletto boots clipped across the cement flooring, and her miniskirt flounced high on her thighs. "Do you see anything that looks like caraway?"

Devon groaned. "Did you ever consider an online dating service? Or the personal ads in the *Sentinel*? You can use my employee discount."

"Do you have any idea how many jerks you meet with those hit-or-miss matchups?" Tasha waved the paper in her face. "This will guarantee us the right guy the first time."

Devon snatched the notes away. "Look me in the eye and say that with a straight face."

Tasha's nose scrunched up, and she stopped walking. "Oh, come on, Dev. Stop being such a downer. What could it hurt to try? We need to shake things up a bit. We're both in a rut."

Devon hooked her thumb into a belt loop of her low-slung jeans and glanced again at Tasha's latest great idea. It looked like nothing more than an exotic recipe.

The hopeful expression on her friend's face made her sigh. Even if she did believe in magic, she really wasn't interested in meeting anyone right now. She knew that only one man could fulfill her needs; no other man could measure up. Still . . .

If it would make Tasha feel better, maybe she should go along with it. Her friend was getting more and more upset about her recurring dream. Whereas Devon looked forward to it, practically *craved* it, Tasha feared it. If this love spell made her friend feel like they were doing something productive, that it would shake Devon's obsession with her silent watcher— what could it hurt?

As long as she got to bed on time . . .

"All right," she gave in. "But is this a generic love spell or can we customize it?" She winked to break the tension. "I want tall, dark, and handsome or there's no deal."

A broad smile lit Tasha's face, and she looped their

arms together. "Now you're talking! Although I've got nothing against blonds . . ."

Together they walked deeper into the greenhouse, looking for the herbs and flowers they needed. The stifling atmosphere made them both want to hurry. The air felt heavy. Clinging. Close. Devon looked around again and realized they were the only customers left. Except for a teenager watering plants at the other end of the building, the entire place was empty.

Dusk was settling upon Solstice, and night wasn't far behind.

"Let's hurry," she said. "We need to be out of here before it gets dark."

"I know. Sorry, but this is the only place I could find that specializes in herbs." Tasha's eyes sparked and she picked up a pot. She scowled when it wasn't what she wanted.

Devon let one eyebrow rise. "How long have you been planning this?"

"Mugwort," Tasha said, blithely ignoring the question and strolling away. "Any idea what it looks like? It sounds like a dermatological problem, but we need some."

Devon hesitated when her gaze landed on a bleeding heart plant, and that feeling of uneasiness once again came over her. She shook it off. The creepy little greenhouse was getting to her. "Let's ask that worker boy."

"Good idea. Hey, cutie pie," Tasha called out to the

teenager. She waved when he gave her a "who me?" look. "Can you help us?"

The boy nearly dropped his hose. Tasha might be tiny, but she packed a punch—especially in that red miniskirt. Never one to let attention pass, she let her hips sway as she strutted down the aisle. Not nearly as overt, Devon followed at more of a distance. Still, the kid's gaze ran a quick sweep over her—and came to a dead stop. Water splashed onto the concrete floor as he gaped. Devon was used to people looking twice at her. The auburn hair and sleek figure she'd inherited from her mother caught as much attention as Tasha's exotic looks.

"Could you tell me where to find these things?" Tasha asked as she passed the teen the paper. Water from the hose poured dangerously close to the toes of her Candie's boots as he reached to take it.

"Oh, gee!" the kid said, embarrassed. He quickly turned to shut off the faucet. "Sorry about that."

"That's all right, sweetie. I'm used to things spurting at me unexpectedly."

Devon's air choked in her throat. She covered it with a cough as Tasha threw her a quick smile.

The boy flushed but tried to summon a sense of professionalism. He looked intently at Tasha's list, but his eyebrows lowered when he read the ingredients.

"Is something the matter?" Devon asked. She couldn't put her finger on what the problem was, but the kid looked uncomfortable. "Don't you have them?"

"We have them." He tugged at his work apron and glanced nervously over his shoulder. "But you'll need to go *in there*."

In there.

Devon and Tasha turned simultaneously. "In there" didn't look very welcoming. A dark, ivy-covered door stood at the very end of the greenhouse. Just looking at it made goose bumps rise at the base of Devon's neck. Something was off here. Very off. "Tasha," she whispered.

They exchanged a look, and Tasha's eyebrows lifted. Devon didn't need to say any more. She didn't get these feelings very often, but when she did, her instincts were uncanny. They'd learned long ago to trust them.

"Thanks, hon," Tasha told the teenager. Taking a deep breath, she once again looped her arm through Devon's. "How bad is it?"

They'd never needed to put a name on "it." "It" was just something that Devon had always had. Call it gut instinct, call it foresight, call it intuition. It didn't matter what name was slapped on it. What did matter was that she was never wrong.

Ever.

This time, though, "it" was different.

"It's weird, but I wouldn't call it bad." Devon instinctively rubbed her stomach. She felt a pull toward that dark, ivy-covered door. She needed to go into that room, but she didn't want to. It was as if two distinct forces were pulling her in opposite directions.

"It's not the good zing?"

Devon shook her head. She got good impressions, too, but even more rarely.

Tasha looked frustrated. "If it's not good and it's not bad, then it must be okay, right? Maybe your swirly belly is just telling you that we're about to have an adventure."

That's all life was to Tasha, one big adventure. Devon wasn't so carefree. "Are you sure this is the only place you can get these herbs?"

Tasha's fingers drummed slowly on the piece of paper. "Well, I suppose I could get them over the Internet."

"Let's do that," Devon said quickly. She pulled away and started to head toward the exit when she noticed the look on Tasha's face. "What?" she demanded.

"We have to perform the spell when the moon is waxing to encourage positive energy. It will take at least a week for the ingredients to be shipped here, and even then it will be too late. And we won't know if they're fresh." Tasha shook off her disappointment and waved her hand airily. "That's okay. If you don't think it's good here, we'll just get everything ready to go for next month. You know I trust you."

Guilt weighed down upon Devon. She didn't want to spoil her friend's fun, yet this seemed like more than just a lark to Tasha. Her friend tended to believe in the metaphysical and all its associated touchy-feely practices.

Devon took a long moment, staring at the door and trying to analyze her reaction.

The door was just a door, but the pull toward it was getting stronger. As much as she wanted to leave, she knew she had to go inside.

"Okay," she finally said. "Since we're already here, we might as well get what you came for."

Tasha brightened visibly. "Are you sure?"

"A month more of those dreams?" Devon reached out and caught her friend's hand. "Maybe this will give me other things to think about."

"Hoo ya, sister! Let's make some magic."

They approached the door, and when Tasha opened it, the hinges gave a long groan. Devon felt cool air rush over her, seeming to beckon her even more. Silently, she stepped forward and entered.

She nearly jumped out of her skin when the heavy door closed behind them.

Feeling defenseless, she looked around quickly. The room was actually a small, well-tended shed. The air was cool and dry, a stark contrast to the tropical greenhouse they'd just left. She blinked and waited for her eyes to adjust to the dim light. Around her, shapes and objects appeared. Overhead, tied bundles of drying plants hung from the ceiling. Netting was carefully placed below to catch any falling seeds. All around her, shelves held flower heads and roots drying on screens. A kitchen-style island stood at the end of the room with knives carefully arranged and pruning scissors at the ready. A compost container held any leftovers to save them for their return to the earth.

Her gaze finally landed upon the wizened old man chopping what looked like parsley with the assurance of a Japanese chef. He paid his visitors no regard, working so fast, his knife seemed a blur. When he finished cutting the herb, he scraped the small bits into a dark jar. Careful to catch every last bit, he filled the container to the brim. Still oblivious to their presence, he dipped his knife in the sink behind him and studiously cleaned it. A lid went tightly onto the jar, and a prepared label was attached. Finally, he looked up.

His watery blue eyes pinned Devon where she stood, concentrating on her so hard, it appeared as if he was trying to read her mind. His heavy white brows drew together until they almost joined.

"What?" she blurted. "Why are you staring at me?"

"Your aura," the old man said in a voice like sandpaper. "Reds and blues and yellows. It's very powerful."

Her mouth went dry. She had no idea how to respond to that.

Tasha quickly stepped into the mix. "Are you the herbalist?" she asked, ever one to get down to brass tacks.

The old man nodded.

"Great," she said brightly.

Too brightly. Devon glanced quickly at her friend. The dim, claustrophobic room was even bothering her. That said something.

Tasha set her list of ingredients onto the island and tucked her shaking hand behind her back. "We're looking for these things."

The old man quickly scanned the list, and his frown deepened. "Are you a practicing Wiccan?" he snapped.

Devon took a step back. How could he know they were planning to perform a spell? Herbs didn't automatically equate to such a thing; they could be cooking, for all he knew. But that was just it. *He knew.* Suddenly, it didn't seem like such a silly, happy-go-lucky thing.

"Uh, no . . . ," Tasha mumbled. She nervously tucked her dark hair behind her ear. "But we'd like—"

"Magic is not something to be trifled with!" The old man pointed a gnarled finger at her, unshaken in his assumptions. "The potential for mishap is too great, especially for those unknowing in the arts. You will not get these items from me."

"But . . . you can't do that!" Tasha gestured around the room. "You're open for business, and I'm willing to pay."

"I said no."

"No?" Tasha St. James had never been refused by

a man before. It stunned her into uncharacteristic silence.

"Will you sell them to *me*?"

The words came out of Devon's mouth without thought. She had no idea why she might be any different from Tasha, but she met his gaze steadily.

His pale blue eyes burned. "Your power is uncontrolled," he declared.

"Yes," she admitted. He knew about her intuition; there was no reason to deny it. But she had to be truthful. The feelings just came over her; she couldn't turn them on and off at will. It had been that way her entire life.

"Yet you have a need to perform this ritual?"

She nodded unequivocally. As soon as she had stepped through that door, Tasha's playful suggestion had become something much more important to her. This was something she needed to do.

"Why?"

Again, it didn't cross her mind to lie. "To find my true love."

The old man didn't laugh. He didn't even blink. "You know he exists."

Unbidden, the vision of dark eyes popped into her head. "Yes."

The herbalist's head dipped in resigned acceptance. "You must be careful. Even simple spells such as this have dark sides if performed without care. You must show your power respect."

"I will," Devon whispered.

She blinked. What was happening here? Fifteen minutes ago, she and Tasha had been footloose and fancy-free. Now, inside this crowded, dark shed, she felt the weight of its seriousness press heavily on her. She needed to get away from this man, away from this place. Night was coming. "Do you have the items on this list? We'd prefer them fresh if you do."

"Yes, yes," he said, finally coming to the conclusion that he couldn't deny her. He moved about carefully as if arthritis besieged his knees. Here and there he toddled, plucking jars off shelves or poking at hanging bundles. "Here's the caraway and the valerian. Now, where did I put that mugwort? Ah yes, here it is."

Devon glanced at the tied bundle curiously. It looked like just another weed. What power did it carry? She hoped Tasha knew what she was doing.

"And here is the cardamom."

Tasha finally took a cautious step forward out of the corner. "Could we have that in oil form?"

The old man lifted an eyebrow at her in irritation, said nothing. He turned to Devon questioningly.

She nodded. "Cardamom oil, please."

"Humpph," he grunted. The item was quickly replaced. "Is that all?"

Devon looked at Tasha out of the corner of her eye. Her friend gave her an almost imperceptible nod.

"I think so," she said.

"No mandrake?"

She looked at him steadily. He certainly had more knowledge than she did.

"It brings fertility, love, and protection."

Fertility was questionable, but protection was a must. She took a deep breath. "Throw it in."

The herbalist sacked up their purchase, but the misgiving in his gaze made Devon shiver. He was scaring her. When he gave her the change for her purchases, his fingers brushed against her palm, and she felt a spark.

So did the old man.

"Power," he muttered under his breath. He raked a gnarled hand through his shock of white hair. "Take the utmost care."

Devon's mouth went dry. She nodded and grabbed the sack. Afraid to turn around, she stepped backward to the door. Tasha was light-years ahead of her. A long groan from the crusty hinges filled the dark room as she yanked open the door. Together, they hurried out into the main greenhouse.

They were greeted by heat and humidity. Devon inhaled in surprise. The warmth was almost sexual in the way it wrapped itself around her. The dampness coated her skin, and the fluorescent lights overhead hummed.

"Let's get out of here," Tasha hissed.

"I'm right behind you."

Just short of a run, they rushed out of the greenhouse to the car. The sun was low on the horizon, and the sky had a hazy, heavy feel to it. The empty parking lot felt lonely as the darkening sky closed in. Tasha started punching the keyless entry button on her key chain before they were halfway there. Neither said a word until they were safe inside with the doors locked.

"What the hell was that?" Tasha asked as she slumped in the driver's seat. Her voice was still unnaturally quiet.

"I'm not sure," Devon said shakily.

"What was going on between the two of you? What was all that mumbo jumbo about power?"

Devon looked at the paper sack in her hands. Hastily, she set it on the floorboard between her feet. She stared at it like a snake in the grass. She couldn't get rid of the pinched feeling between her shoulder blades. "Let's not go back there again."

"Duh! That old geezer wigged me out!" Tasha's energy returned with a rush. She plugged her key into the ignition and fired up the engine. "This potion better work."

Devon glanced at her friend. "You think we should still do it?"

Tasha stilled. "You think we shouldn't?"

The energy settled in Devon's gut once again. She had a feeling it wouldn't be going away for a long, long time. She rubbed her hand in circles over her stomach and glanced at the greenhouse. With a long exhale, she settled back into the bucket seat. "I think we have to."

Absently, she traced her finger along the edge of the ingredient list. It drew her, made her curious as to what the love spell could really do . . .

His face. She just wanted to see his face. Touch it, if that wasn't too much to ask.

She shoved the piece of paper back into Tasha's purse. She should be laughing off this whole experience. This was just for fun. There was no such thing as magic. That sack contained a bunch of harmless weeds. They'd make weed soup, say some silly rhymes, cough over incense fumes, and have a story to tell afterward.

It was nothing.

"Why am I so afraid to do this?" she whispered.

"Are you afraid the spell is going to backfire?"

Devon bit her lip. "No. I'm afraid it's going to work."

Two

The sky was dark and the moon was rising by the time Tasha collected all her supplies. Excitement radiated from her as she hurried to and fro, making sure everything was ready. Devon watched quietly from the kitchen table. Hers was more of a nervous energy. She couldn't shake the feelings she'd experienced at the greenhouse. The old man's pale eyes were burned into her memory.

"Take the utmost care," he'd warned.

She watched every move her friend made.

A large pot of boiling water was on the stove. The herbs from the greenhouse had been sorted but otherwise left untouched. Rose petals from her backyard stood at the ready in a small bowl. A CD of nature sounds was playing in the background, and the directions for the spell were taped onto the cupboard above the stove. From what she could tell, everything was being prepared with respect and diligence.

She let out a long breath. That old man had really gotten to her.

At last, Tasha stepped back and surveyed everything. With a glance outside the window at the moon, she decided it was time. "Hit the lights, Dev."

Devon pushed back her chair and stood on unsteady legs. Her hand quivered as she doused the overhead light. Darkness fell over the room like a thick blanket, but she welcomed it. For her, darkness meant solace. Pleasure. She concentrated on the feelings to calm her nerves.

Tasha struck a match and carefully lit three candles. "Ready?" she asked.

Devon crossed the room and stood beside her friend at the stove. "What do we need to do?"

"We start with the cardamom oil." With a bow of her head, Tasha reached for the small bottle. Upon popping the cork, a sweet but pungent smell filled the air. "Give me your wrist."

Devon stuck out her right hand. She watched intently as her friend rubbed the oil onto the point where her wrist creased against the base of her palm.

"Cardamom is an earth element. It will make you more receptive to love. Open yourself to it and it will draw passion into your life."

Sitting so close to the stove, the oil had been warmed. The sweet aroma filled Devon's senses, and she felt herself relax, become more accepting. When Tasha was done, she reached for the bottle and reciprocated by rubbing the oil onto her friend's wrist.

With a solemn look on her face, Tasha passed her a wooden spoon. "Stir in a clockwise motion, the motion of the sun, to invoke blessings. I'll add the ingredients."

Devon nodded and began to stir the boiling pot. Steam curled into the air, reminding her of the humidity in the greenhouse. The sensuality came back with a rush.

"The rose," Tasha said. "An element of water. Made from Aphrodite's blood, it will bring us luck in love."

The petals puckered as the hot water seeped into their pores. Devon watched, entranced, as they closed upon themselves and were pulled under.

"Cloves." Three soft plops sounded in the dark room as Tasha added the pungent flavoring to the mix. "An element of fire. It will bring about cleansing and encourage romance."

Devon watched the cloves swirl around the bottom of the pot as the roses petals tried to catch up. The flames from the candles reflected off the surface of the water. An element of fire and an element of water. It seemed almost poetic.

The paper bag crinkled as Tasha pulled out the caraway seeds. A spicy, bittersweet scent filled the room.

"An element of air, meant to bring awareness and devotion. Then mugwort, an earth element to ensure stamina."

"Add the mandrake," Devon said. "The herbalist said it would bring love and protection."

She watched as the pot began to fill. The clashing aromas filled the kitchen, but she began to cough when Tasha opened the last sealed plastic bag. "Oh my God, what is that?"

Tasha held the bag as far away from her as she could but clamped her other hand over her mouth and nose. "Valerian," she wheezed. "Holy balls. That smells like a men's locker room."

Devon kept stirring but buried her face in the crook of her other arm. "Are you sure we need that? We've got at least one of each element."

Tasha looked at her forlornly. "It's the most important part."

"What's it bring?"

"Lust."

Devon sighed. "Toss it in, but make it fast."

The smell dissipated—along with the distraction—as the hot water was absorbed into the pungent root. Devon watched as the potion quickly reached its boiling point again. The surface began to roll, and she couldn't take her eyes off it. Behind her, the CD moved on to the whoosh of a windstorm.

Suddenly, the tingle she'd experienced in her belly earlier came back.

Only this time it was a pang.

Tasha held a candle up to the invocation. "We'll say it together, repeating it three times."

"Okay," Devon said, letting out a nervous puff of air. Light and shadows were dancing across the poem, enticing her, daring her.

Tasha nodded and they began.

Earth, Water, Wind, and Fire,
Lead me to my heart's desire.
Bring passion, love, and romance
Before the waxing moon has passed.

Halfway through the first stanza, Devon felt an odd sensation. The pang in her belly was pulsing, sending an uproar through her entire body. Her fingers clenched the wooden spoon as she stirred mechanically, but her fingertips stung as the sensation flowed outward. Her toes curled as the feeling crept down her legs.

By the second time through the incantation, she was feeling light-headed. Tasha's eyes widened as she took notice. She reached for the spoon, but Devon's hand was clenched so tightly, she couldn't let go. Tasha wrapped her hand over the top of hers, and together they stirred.

"Earth, Water, Wind, and Fire," Devon said for the third time.

The words reverberated in her head. Aromas filled

her nose until she could almost taste them. The flow of energy consumed her entire body until she thought she might combust.

"Lead me to my heart's desire!"

The wind on the CD picked up, and her hair whipped around her shoulders. The room started to spin and the flames on the candles lengthened, reaching for the sky.

All of a sudden, she saw colors on the wall—and her dream man's eyes! She could almost make out his features . . . the shape of his form . . .

"Bring passion, love, and romance before the waxing moon has passed."

A loud bang split the room.

The vision vanished, and Devon's knees gave out. "Ahhhh!"

Tasha spun around. The spoon clattered into the pot as Devon started to go down.

"Cedric!" Tasha exclaimed.

Devon clung to the counter and reached out for a chair. She pulled it to her before she could drop to the floor. She heard the clip of the dog's nails. He let out a soft whimper, instinctively afraid of the sensations floating on the air, but she was in no shape to comfort him. Leaning over, she dropped her head into her hands.

"Silly dog," Tasha said with a nervous laugh. She leaned down to ruffle his fur. "Whew! I think you scared us as much as we scared you."

She turned on the overhead light and Devon squeezed her eyes shut. After the soft glow of candlelight, the fluorescent light seemed inhumanely harsh.

"Oh, my God!" Tasha said. "Did you feel that sizzle in the air? Was that amazing or what?"

"Mmm." Devon cautiously lifted her head and when the room didn't spin, slowly sat up. She rubbed her aching temples. She felt as if she'd just run a marathon.

"Something was definitely working there. I could feel it." Tasha spun around in a circle with her arms lifted. "Look at Cedric—he can feel it, too. Can't ya, poochie?"

Cedric let out a soft yelp and waddled over to Devon. Reflexively, she reached down to rub him behind the ears. He belonged to the neighbors, but after five years, he'd yet to learn where his home was. She hadn't had the heart to nail shut the old doggy door to keep him away. She opened the lower cupboard door and his tail began to wag as she pulled out a Milk-Bone.

Tasha's heels were nearly doing a tap dance as she moved about the kitchen. "I mean . . . Wow! I had high hopes, but nothing like that. Did you see the flames, Dev? That's got to be a good thing."

Devon wasn't so sure. Her skin felt overly sensitive, *energized,* but she was so tired. So very, very tired.

She pushed her hair over her shoulder but stopped midmotion as the wooziness came over her again.

"I've got to go check this out," Tasha said giddily. "Maya said she was going to Trusdale's tonight. Maybe I'll join her."

Devon looked at her friend in stupefaction. She was planning on hitting the town? She couldn't be serious.

Tasha smoothed her miniskirt. "I hadn't planned on going out. Do you think I look okay for Mr. Right?"

Her wardrobe was a fashionista's wet dream. "You look fantastic and you know it."

"Makeup," Tasha said, already moving on to the next problem. She grabbed her purse and was out of the room like a shot. Even for her, she was on a high.

Devon, meanwhile, was at an all-time energy low. She rubbed the sweet spot behind Cedric's ear and looked blankly across the room. With the lights on, her kitchen seemed so normal. Had she imagined what had just happened? She could have sworn that she'd seen wisps of color dancing on the walls.

She could have sworn she'd almost seen his face . . .

Her belly squeezed in aftershock. Energy *had* whipped through the room. She'd felt it from the tips of her toes to the top of her head.

What in God's name had they just done?

Tasha bounced back into the room looking fresh

and gorgeous. She stopped when she saw Devon's pale face. "Oh, honey. Are you okay?"

Devon raked a hand through her hair and took stock. "I think I inhaled too much of that valerian."

Tasha reached out and pressed the back of her hand against her forehead. "You're warm."

"I'm fine. I just overheated standing over the stove."

One of Tasha's eyebrows lifted. She wasn't as oblivious as she sometimes pretended to be. "It wasn't the stale sock odor, Dev. Something just happened. You know it, and I know it. We just worked some potent magic here."

Devon frowned. She wanted to deny it. There was no sane way they could have set anything into motion by throwing some dead plants into a pot and saying a simple rhyme. Still, a power had swept through the room. She didn't know if it had been magic, but it had definitely been something.

Not knowing what that "something" was worried her. "Whatever we did, I hope we did it right."

Tasha brushed off the warning. "There's only one way to find out. Want to go with me?"

Devon slowly pushed herself to her feet. "I think I'll just go to bed."

"Are you sure?"

She felt like she could sleep for days. Walking over to the stove, she fished the wooden spoon out of the pot and put it on a spoon rest. "You go ahead. I'll clean up."

Never one to look a gift horse in the mouth, Tasha headed for the door. "I'll call you tomorrow to let you know what happened," she called over her shoulder.

Devon heard the car engine firing almost before the back door slammed. Wearily, she leaned over to blow out the candles. Cedric loitered at her feet, sniffing the air in confusion.

"It's valerian. Don't worry, I'm working on getting rid of it."

Cleaning up the kitchen took the last bit of energy Devon had. By the time she bagged up the leftover herbs, rinsed out the pot, and stuck it in the dishwasher, she was nearly asleep on her feet. She heard the bang of the doggy door as Cedric left. Even he could tell the fun was over. Turning off the CD, she headed toward the stairs. It took everything she had to lift her heavy legs as she climbed the steps to her bedroom.

She changed into a nightie and slid under the sheets. The crisp cotton abraded her still-sensitive skin, but her fatigued muscles relaxed as the mattress took her weight. She couldn't remember being so tired in her life.

It even overrode the anticipation humming through her veins—the anticipation she was trying to ignore . . .

The room started to go out of focus before she even closed her eyes. By the time her head settled against the pillow, she was asleep.

. . .

He watched her. Again.

Devon could feel his presence at her bedside. She could sense his warmth; discern his heat. She rolled onto her back as the familiar ache settled low in her belly. The need was getting worse. Each night, it intensified, growing sharper and clearer. If it weren't satisfied soon, it would turn on her. Overtake her.

She shifted restlessly. The cotton sheets chafed her, the contact cool and impersonal. She ached for the brush of a warm hand, the caress of a soft mouth.

His mouth. His hands.

With a groan, she tossed her pillow onto the floor. She stretched uncomfortably, trying to find a way to ease her torment. And it was torment—this never-fulfilled desire.

It had to stop. One way or the other.

Slowly, she opened her eyes.

It was the same as it had always been. The room was dark, save for the moonlight slanting through the window by her head. Yet as she listened carefully, she could hear someone else breathing.

Her pulse began to thud.

Hesitantly, her gaze shifted upward. Dark, fathomless eyes stared back at her. The distress in them nearly matched her own.

A soft whimper left her throat. Why must it always be this way?

She tried to lift her hand and her arm drifted upward, almost weightless. She turned her hand to look at her palm, amazed when her muscles effortlessly obeyed.

Freedom! The crushing lethargy was gone. She was free to move!

She surged upright. She heard his sudden intake of breath and felt the air about her shift as he stepped backward.

"No! Don't leave me. Not this time."

Kneeling on the mattress, she hesitantly reached for him.

And found him. Warm and real under the gentle touch of her palm.

She watched in wonder as the moonlit haze cleared. The fog dissipated as particles assembled. Energy and matter collected at the point where she touched his cheek, and a rugged face appeared. Devon froze, afraid to move, afraid to breathe. She didn't want to do anything accidentally to make this all go away. In awe, she stared into those dark eyes.

He let out a shuddering breath at the feel of her touch, and suddenly, he was *there*. Tall, muscled, and *alive*.

Her hungry gaze took in every inch of him. He had dark hair to match the dark eyes, a wicked slash of a mouth, and wide shoulders. Her gaze drifted lower. Good God, he was ripped! Unable to stop herself, she slid her hand down to his muscular chest. She understood now why she'd always been able to feel his heat. He generated it like a furnace. Entranced, she watched as her fingers traced the lines of his body. She'd imagined him for so long. Now he was here, and he was a thousand times better than anything her imagination had ever conjured.

"Devon?" he asked, his voice hoarse. His heart thundered under her palm. Shock shone in his eyes as his body went on the alert, but he didn't pull back. Instead, his gaze dropped to where she touched him.

Hearing her name on those lips sent a shiver down her spine. "I finally found you."

Confusion wrinkled his brow. "But what . . . How?"

"I wished it," she whispered. "I made the dream continue."

Her inquisitive fingers began to slide down to the well-delineated muscles of his six-pack abs. Her senses were bombarded with him. She'd always been able to sense him. Now she could see him. Touch him. Hear him.

She wanted to taste.

She swayed forward, but he drew back.

"What dream?" His dark eyes were lit with fire. She could feel their heat as he searched her face.

"This dream. My dream of us."

She slowly reached for him again, and this time he didn't stop her. Her fingers shook as she traced the line of his jaw. "I dream of you every night. You stand over me while I sleep."

He stilled. "You've watched me?"

Her lips twitched. "I've watched *you* watch *me*."

His muscles tensed, and he gradually stepped

away from her. Putting the wall at his back, he quickly searched the room. When his gaze finally landed on her again, it was hot. Blistering hot, yet guarded.

"What's happening here?" he asked, his voice tight.

Devon could see his wariness. She felt his desire more.

She slipped off the bed. "Why are you so upset? I thought you'd want this."

He froze. Shock lit his face as he looked first at her and then back to the bed.

He caught her then, pulling her to him protectively. She gasped aloud. His touch on her flesh sizzled. He felt it, too. For a long moment, his hands lingered. Finally, he looked into her eyes. "Devon," he whispered, "how did you 'make the dream continue'?"

God, she loved his hands on her. "The power of suggestion," she purred.

He caught her chin. "Red, what did you do?"

She looked into those eyes that had tempted her for so long. "A love spell."

Unbidden, the spaghetti strap of her nightie slid down her shoulder.

The glide of silk was inexorable. They both watched, unable to stop it as it slipped over his fingers, brushed against his knuckles, and bared the upper curve of her breast.

The air in the room thickened as they both went dead still.

Devon lifted her gaze slowly to his face. The muscles in his throat worked as he stared at her. Hungrily. Achingly. *Devotedly*. Desire hit her so hard, her knees nearly buckled. Those were the dark eyes she knew. This was the connection she'd always felt between them.

He looked at her helplessly.

Then turning his hand, he caught the teal blue strap and slowly tugged it down the rest of the way. Devon stood there, breathing fast, as the silk rasped over her curves. She felt the roughness of the lace trim brush over her before the material dropped to her waist.

Her breaths came harder, her nipples peaking as he looked at her. Still, she wasn't ready when his hand cupped her. The sensation was jolting. The heat. The intimacy. Her nipple speared into his palm, and electricity shot right down to her core.

"Mmm," she hummed. His touch was firm and possessive, just like she'd known it would be. She shifted closer as he began to knead and mold her. It felt so good. *So good*.

She brushed her lips against his chest, wanting to touch him back. She wrapped her arms around him and shuddered when her nakedness pressed against his hot, hard flesh.

Skin on skin. It felt so real.

He let out a groan, and his fingers caught in her hair. Pulling her head back, he sealed his mouth over hers. Devon felt a thrill when he pushed his tongue deep. She let her tongue dance with his, and the arousal that had lurked beneath the surface came surging forward.

And it was *insane*.

A low moan left her throat when his steely arms came around her. Wanting to get closer, she wrapped her leg sinuously about his waist. He caught her bottom and lifted her to him.

"Ah!" she cried out when she settled against him.

Her hungry pussy was riding right against his hardening cock. Instinctively, she swirled her hips.

He groaned. "You are so beautiful."

Turning, he set her on the dresser. The coolness of the wood pressed against her bottom as he slid her forward, keeping their bodies pressed tight.

"Bewitching," he whispered. His gaze dropped to her naked breast, now at mouth level.

Devon arched before his lips even touched her. His tongue dragged over her nipple, and she let out a cry. He tugged the sensitive peak deeper into his hot mouth.

"Oh, God," she moaned as he began to suckle.

The tug was inexorable. Pleasure speared right down to her core. Her back bowed, and she felt his hands tugging at the strap on her other shoulder. He turned his attention to her other nipple, and she bucked when he gave it a soft nip.

"Dreamer," she moaned. Her head rolled against the mirror behind her.

Need was roiling inside her, and she pressed her

mound more fiercely against his stiff cock. It was locked up against her tight, only a few layers of thin fabric separating his hard flesh from her sensitive core.

"Devon," he said hoarsely. She squirmed as his hand slid up her thigh. It went right up under her nightie and into her panties.

"Hurry," she begged. "Please hurry."

Reaching between their straining bodies, she grasped for his pajama bottoms. The tie slipped out of reach. Opening her eyes, she looked for the string.

A flash of red in her peripheral vision distracted her.

She looked over her dream man's shoulder and froze.

They weren't alone.

There, on the bed in the moonlight, was a woman. A woman with long legs, auburn hair, and a teal nightie.

Devon stared, unable to process the image. Her thighs tightened around her lover's waist.

"What is that?" she asked, dread building up inside her chest.

He turned quickly, putting her behind him as he scanned the room. "What? Where?"

Devon could hardly look at it. "The bed. *Who is that?*"

He glanced at her cautiously. "That's you, Red."

Revulsion rolled in her stomach. Her dream had just taken a sick turn.

"But I'm . . . she looks dead."

He eased back up to her. "You're fine. It's all right."

Devon glanced over his shoulder and shuddered. Her twin on the bed was motionless. She couldn't even see her breathing. The moonlight made her skin a deathly shade of pale and her hand fell limply over the side of the bed. Devon quickly turned her face away.

Her dream man's erection still throbbed against her, but his touch was gentle. "Relax," he said, cupping the back of her head.

She couldn't. Everything was too real. His touch . . . his scent . . . *that corpse* . . .

Devon knew she should have believed that tingle. She'd known it wasn't good.

"Just close your eyes, Sexy Red." He gently tugged her clothes up, covering her nakedness. He let out a shuddering breath. "Go back to sleep. Everything will be all right when you wake up."

"I *am* asleep."

He hesitated. "Then just . . . let go."

That's what she'd been trying to do. She kept her gaze averted from the bed and took calming breaths. Why wasn't she waking up? Why weren't *either* of them waking up?

Her dream man rubbed her back, his body nearly as tense as hers. Finally, he swore and gathered her up into his arms.

"What are you doing?" she squeaked. Her fingers bit into his shoulders as he swung her around.

"Putting things right. You need to go back."

"What?" Her heart leapt into her throat when he started carrying her toward the bed. Toward death. "No!"

She started to struggle in his arms, but he was big. Those muscles she'd admired were strong and he was determined. Her head snapped toward the bed. He was carrying her closer and closer to her lifeless form. "Stop!" she yelled, kicking hard.

"I won't hurt you, Sexy Red. Trust me."

He started to lower her, and panic exploded inside her chest. She screamed, but he pressed her down onto the mattress.

"Let it happen," he said, his jaw tight and his eyes full of anguish.

She lurched upward, but his hand touched her brow. Almost at once, his form started to fade. The room began to disappear.

"Dream, Devon," his voice said, trailing away. "Dream better dreams of me."

Three

Devon awakened the next morning with a start. Gasping for air, she sat straight up in bed. Her gaze flitted about the room as her racing heart pounded in her ears.

No, that pounding was on her front door.

She kicked the twisted sheet off. Her legs weren't quite steady as she got out of bed, but she grabbed her robe and headed toward the stairs. The knocking intensified, and she hurried to look out the peephole.

"Tasha!" She yanked open the door. "What are you doing here? Is something wrong?"

Tasha's eyes narrowed as she looked Devon over from head to toe. "No! Don't tell me. Ruffled hair. Pink cheeks. Lingerie. *You* got lucky last night? You said you were staying home!"

Devon caught her friend by the arm and pulled her inside, happy for the company. She had to admit it; for once Tasha wasn't outstyling her. Her friend was dressed in an old T-shirt, shorts, and slippers. Her pillow was clutched protectively to her chest, and dark circles underlined her eyes. Devon raised one eyebrow. "Did you stay out all night?"

"I wish." Tasha hugged the pillow to her chest. "I'm exhausted. I'm looking for some peace and quiet."

"What's wrong with your place?"

Her friend's lips flattened. "I have a new neighbor who thought it would be a good idea to move in at six o'clock this morning."

Ouch. Devon could commiserate. She'd had one of the worst night's sleeps of her life. "Come on in."

"Are you sure I'm not interrupting?" Unabashedly, Tasha tried to peek over her shoulder. "Is he still here?"

"He who?"

"*He.* The guy who made you look so well tumbled."

Devon blanched and couldn't help but glance up toward her bedroom. Fear was still crawling along her nerve endings, and her brain was having trouble distinguishing reality from nightmare. Yet as warm and alive as her dream man had seemed, she knew he wasn't real. None of it had been real.

Thank God.

"Nobody's here but me."

"Then what are you still doing in bed? It's almost nine. You never sleep this late." Tasha walked around her in a slow circle. "Your hair's wild, and you're breathing hard." Her eyes narrowed as she came to stand in front of Devon again. "Did I interrupt your own personal playtime?"

"Stop it. I had a nightmare."

"Oh, sorry." Moving over to the couch, Tasha tossed her pillow up against the armrest and lay down. "Was it bad?"

With those three simple words, it all came rushing back. The need. The thrill.

The horror.

Devon sank into her favorite chair and tucked her feet up close on the hassock. Her robe draped open around her. "I haven't had one that bad for a long time."

"What was it about?"

She hesitated. "The same as always . . ."

"Not that again."

No, this time had been different. She pushed her hair out of her face, and her fingers caught on a snag. She must look the way she felt. Disheveled. Out of control. *Wild.*

"I saw him."

Tasha's head perked up off the pillow. "The invisible dream man?"

Devon nodded and a shiver passed from the top of her head down to her toes.

"But it was bad?" Tasha scowled. "Don't tell me. He was an ogre. Warts on the face. A missing ear . . ."

"He was gorgeous."

Her friend's forehead rumpled. "Then what was the problem?"

Devon's throat tightened. The dream was as vivid now in the bright morning sunshine as it had been in the black of the night. "I dreamed I died."

That made Tasha sit straight up. "Oh, my God! What did he do to you?"

"Dream," Devon said lightly, trying to ease the tension. "Remember?"

"I know. That's why I'm freaking out!" Her friend's face had paled. "Dreams about death are bad, Dev. If you dream you die . . . it means you will."

"That's a myth," Devon said quickly. Too quickly. "It means I'm facing a transition, some change in my life."

"Well, I don't like it."

Neither did she.

Devon shifted uncomfortably. She could still feel her dream man's touch at her breast, taste his kisses on her tongue, and hear his pleasured sighs in her ears. That part of the dream had been perfect, idyllic, but the uglier moments just wouldn't go away. She could still see herself lying so still. Feel him carrying her toward the bed . . . pressing her down . . .

"And I really don't like that your dream changed right after we did that spell." Tasha's nervous gaze swung toward her. "You weren't thinking about him when we performed it, were you?"

Devon couldn't quite meet that look.

"Devon!" Tasha popped off the couch and began pacing. She raked both hands through her long hair, then spun around. "Tell me this dream. All of it."

Devon wanted to kick herself. Hadn't she sworn just last night that she wouldn't worry Tasha anymore with this? Her friend was sensitive, and right now she looked as wired as Devon felt. Maybe more. "It's not what you're thinking—he didn't hurt me. Please sit down. Everything's okay."

A stubborn look hardened Tasha's jaw, but she took a deep breath and headed back to the couch. She sat down stiffly. "If he didn't do it, how did you die?"

"I'm not even sure I did," Devon said gently. "I just saw myself lying on the bed; it was like I was on the outside looking in. Really, I'm probably making too big a deal of it."

"What do your dream books say about it?"

"I don't know, but I'll look it up." Devon cocked her head. It was difficult trying to ease her friend's mind when hers was still spinning so rapidly. "There could be a silver lining to this. I'm pretty sure my recurring dream is done."

"And this is better?"

"He *was* really hot."

Tasha threw her a sidelong look. "How hot?"

"When he kissed me, it could have peeled the paint off the walls."

Even with the darkness of the dream still pressing on her, she hadn't forgotten that. Those eyes—all he'd had to do was look at her and she'd gotten wet. And his body. She'd seen gym rats who weren't that chiseled. His touch, though. She couldn't get the sensation off her skin. His hands on her had felt electric. Powerful.

Something slid against her shoulder, and she turned to see the strap of her nightie fall over the curve of her shoulder and down her arm. With a sharp inhale, she yanked it back into place. "So how was Trusdale's?" she asked hurriedly. "Any good-looking guys there?"

"No," Tasha said grumpily. "It was a waste of time."

Devon frowned. Tasha always had fun at the club. She was the classic social butterfly who could and would talk to anybody. If talking was a no go, she could dance any of those silly blond pop stars under the table.

"The place was filled with duds." With a dramatic flounce, Tasha laid back down. "I met a close talker with such bad breath, he could have wilted that valerian at ten paces. Then there was the winker. He might not have been half bad if he hadn't been cross-eyed. I couldn't tell if he was winking at me or the barmaid."

Devon leaned her head back against the comfy cushions. "You didn't expect that spell to work overnight, did you?"

Her friend threw her a narrowed look. "I'm beginning to think we never should have cast that thing at all."

Devon couldn't argue with that. "So what time did you get home?"

"Maya and I closed the place down, hoping that Mr. Right would make an appearance. He didn't."

"But your new neighbor showed up at six?"

The growl was barely muffled by the pillow.

"Did you say something to him?"

"I would have, but I didn't know which one he was. There were four of them clomping around the place, bumping up against the walls." Tasha let out a big yawn. "Isn't that illegal on a Sunday morning?"

"If it's not, it should be." Devon yawned too but determinedly pushed herself to her feet. She'd had enough of sleep. "You're welcome to nap here. I'm going down to the *Sentinel* for a few hours."

"I didn't think you were working this weekend."

Walking over to the window, Devon pulled down the shades she'd been too tired to deal with last night. "I'm not, but we've got that new editor coming in. I want to clean up my desk and make a good first impression."

"But you're a photographer. You're never at your desk."

"Which is why it's always so messy. Sleep tight. We'll go to lunch when I get back."

Tasha's head lifted from the pillow. "Are you sure you're all right?"

"I'm fine."

Although she had to admit, she was still a little shaken. She turned and climbed the stairs. She just wanted to keep busy, to keep herself from thinking. Walking into her bedroom, her gaze fell on the bed.

She couldn't do that here.

Sunday breakfast at IHOP was a family tradition—and obligation. Cael listened with only half an ear as conversations bounced around the table like pinballs. It was always like this when he and his brothers got together. Loud. Boisterous. Ten different conversations could be going on at once, but everybody managed to keep up. Except today. Today, he was distracted.

He glanced around the table, drumming his fingers against his thigh. Only four of his brothers had shown up. Tony's hair was still wet. He'd most likely come straight from the gym. Derek, as always, was wearing a business suit. Serious and quiet, he mainly listened. Conversely, Wes and Zane chattered away like magpies. Two of the youngest in the family, they were also two of the quickest to react.

Cael wished more had come. Sometimes it was easier to hide in a crowd.

His fingers stilled. Then again, this wasn't something he could hide. As much as he wanted to keep what had happened last night private, he knew he couldn't. This weekly gathering was as much a business meeting as it was a social gathering.

And today, the Dream Wreakers had serious business to attend to.

"Aren't you hungry, hon?" Sally asked as she put more syrup on the table.

The IHOP waitresses were used to the weekly invasion. Although it meant more work, none of the women ever complained. By now, they were used to the noise and requests for more coffee and extra bacon. The extra tips were undoubtedly nice, and Cael had a sneaking suspicion that family genetics played some part, too. Sometimes it didn't hurt being descended from Greek gods.

Most of the time, though, it was more responsibility, worry, and danger than he liked.

"I'm done." He sat back to let her take his plate. The food he'd already eaten was sitting like a rock in the pit of his stomach.

"Are you kidding me?" Tony said. His fork was quick as it stabbed a sausage link and saved it from going to waste. "What's wrong with you?"

"Nothing." Just responsibility and worry bearing down on his shoulders. Cael reached for his coffee, but caffeine was the last thing he needed. He went for his water instead. "Let's just get started."

Wes made a face. "Somebody got up on the wrong side of the bed."

"Obviously an *empty* bed," Zane muttered.

"Enough," Cael said. They were here to work. Surreptitiously, he looked around the restaurant, making sure the waitresses were busy and people at surrounding tables weren't paying too close attention. "Let's start with status reports."

Tony shrugged a muscled shoulder. "I've got nothing to report. My charges are all sleeping well and dreaming fine."

The comment might have seemed strange to anyone else. Crazy. Out there. Cael simply nodded.

They were the Oneiroi, modern-day Dream Wreakers. Sons of Nyx and bestowers of dreams.

An army of them circled the globe, watching over charges assigned to their care—sleepers who didn't even know they were there.

"Wes?" Cael called.

His younger brother sat up straight, looking earnest. He'd only recently come up into their ranks, but he took his nighttime duties seriously. "Are you sure it's okay to be talking here?"

Cael's glance sliced to the family at the booth closest to them. It was clear they were intent on making it to a late church service. All their concentration was on their pancakes. "You can talk."

Wes hesitated. "I've got two charges who are dealing with insomnia," he finally confessed.

Everyone murmured. As frustrating as it could be for them, insomnia was outside their purview. They weren't Sandmen. It was only once humans fell asleep that they could do their work, helping their charges dream.

"I'm worried about one," Wes admitted. "He's been having trouble for a while. I've tried to sneak in there, but he's only getting to stage two of the sleep cycle."

"Don't force it," Derek warned.

Sleepers went through various stages over the course of the night, gradually progressing into deeper and deeper slumber. Stage four provided the best rest for their bodies, but REM sleep restored their minds.

Unfortunately, humans couldn't dream without Dream Wreakers' help.

"Watch him closely," Cael instructed. "Let us know how he's doing next week."

He turned to the next in line and braced himself. "Zane?"

A salacious smile lit his brother's face. "I've got this woman who's having dreams like you wouldn't believe. Three truckers, an ice storm, and—"

Cael's fingers tightened around his glass. "Do you have anything relevant to tell us?"

"Man, you are wound tight today." Zane rocked onto the back legs of his chair. "I've got a bed wetter. Poor kid."

Cael relented. Kids were tough. "He'll grow out of it."

"Yeah, well he'd better soon. He's taking the embarrassment hard, and his dreams are killing me."

That was always the hardest part of their job: watching those they cared for struggle. It wasn't the Dream Wreakers' job to guide their charges' dreams, but standing back as they tried to find their own way could be hell.

For a moment, Cael's concentration slipped. Was that what Devon had been doing last night? Trying to find her way?

"My charges are on schedule," Derek said without prompting.

Cael glanced over to find his reserved brother watching him like a hawk. One eyebrow lifted in question, and Cael felt pinned. Shit. Why did the one family member with an IQ of 160 have to show up this morning?

"Is there something bothering *you* that we should know about?"

Glances flicked their way. Derek was their steadying force, their rock, *The Machine*. Not much got by him, and when he asked questions, they all paid attention.

Cael was grateful when the late churchgoers suddenly decided it was time to leave. They slid noisily out of their booth, and all his brothers quickly fell into cover mode. The reprieve didn't last nearly long enough. The moment the family was out of earshot, Derek leaned forward again. "Did something happen last night?"

Cael's fingers bit into his glass so hard, he heard it crack. He set the tumbler down before it could shatter.

He resented having to lay his personal life out for everyone to see. He didn't give a damn if this was his family. What had happened between him and Devon should remain between the two of them.

And it would have, if she hadn't broken the laws of paraphysics.

"Devon Bradshaw," he said, his throat feeling like sandpaper.

Zane snorted. "Should've known. Sexy Red. You are so hung up on her, man."

Cael let the comment pass. "She saw me last night."

Four confused gazes turned toward him.

Tony cleared his throat. "I think you've got that backward, bro. *You* see *her*. You touch her forehead. Dreams ensue. That's how it works."

Cael shook his head slowly. "Last night in her bedroom, she stood up and came right at me. *She talked to me.*"

The front legs of Zane's chair came down with a bang. Humans should never be able to see them, much less interact. They worked from the dream realm, a parallel universe that hid them from sleepers.

"You need to explain yourself, big brother. Pronto."

Cael took a deep breath. Leaning forward, he braced his elbows against his knees and clasped his hands together. Automatically, everyone at the table leaned forward to hear. With a glance at Sally cleaning up the nearby booth, he dropped his voice. "Devon broke through the dream barrier last night. She came into our realm."

Four big bodies pulled away in shock.

"No way."

"That can't happen."

"But it did." He clasped his hands together so tightly, his fingers turned white. *"She touched me."*

"When you say 'touched,' do you mean—"

"Zip it, Zane."

"I don't know whether to congratulate you or kick you into next week," Derek said icily. He waited until Sally scooped up her tip and walked away before folding his fist atop the table. "I know you like the woman, but you're not supposed to pull her through like that. Do you have any idea what the implications could be? The side effects? It's our job to keep the balance!"

Cael's head whipped to the side. "I didn't have anything to do with it. She came through all by herself. I was just a stunned bystander."

Right up until she'd plastered herself against him. He'd been real quick to get in the game then. All that red hair, that soft white skin, those never-ending legs . . . There was only so much a guy could take.

"But how?" Wes demanded. "How did she make the jump?"

Cael grimaced. "It looked like some form of astral projection. Kind of like what we do."

At night, while they slept, Dream Wreakers' spirits split from their corporeal bodies so they could travel freely about the dream realm, tending to sleepers. Seeing Devon do it, though, had been downright disturbing.

"But why would she do that?" Wes pressed. "What could make her break through? What reason could she possibly have?"

Silence fell over the table. Unfortunately, there were many possibilities—nearly all of them bad.

"She did it to get to me," Cael said quietly. "She performed a spell so she could find me."

"What kind of spell?" Derek asked, his voice tight.

Christ. He hadn't wanted to get into this. "A love spell."

Wes took one look at Zane and they both burst out laughing. Even Derek had to fight a smile pulling at his lips.

"A love spell?" Zane said, catching his breath. "God, that's priceless."

Cael didn't think it was funny.

Devon had crossed an impossible barrier to get to him. Just the idea of it was enough to get his blood pumping. She'd been so soft and responsive in his arms, totally unabashed in her needs. It was his fantasy come to life.

But could that have been the point? To throw him off? To distract his attention enough to make him vulnerable?

"She said she'd sensed me standing over her. *Months ago*."

That stopped Zane's rendition of "Love Potion Number Nine" fast.

Tony's face turned serious. "You think there's something else pulling her strings?"

"I don't know," Cael said.

The possibility made his stomach pull tight. His kind had to be vigilant. There were forces out there that would love to see the Dream Wreakers destroyed or even just weakened. They'd use any trick they could think of to catch them off their guard.

Including seduction.

Frustrated, Cael threw his napkin onto the table. "Has anyone heard any rumblings from the other side? Maybe she's been possessed by a dark spirit or a poltergeist."

Stray spirits lurked in the night, searching for new homes or twisted entertainment. The possibility that they might be using Devon made him want to punch something. "Maybe they found out about my . . . connection to her."

Zane shook his head. "Things have been pretty quiet."

"What about the Night Terrors? Are they on the move?"

Everyone tensed. Of all their enemies, the Night Terrors were the worst.

Tony played with the saltshaker. He never could keep still when he got nervous. "The Lunatics are coming to power, but that's nothing unusual. The full moon is in a few days."

"But I haven't heard of *them* doing anything like this before," Wes said. "They make people wacky. They don't pull them through dimensions."

"What about a Somnambulist?" Zane said. "That could explain her walking and talking."

"I've never known one of those parasites to take a sleepwalker into the dream realm," Derek said. "I don't know if they even can."

"It wasn't a Somnambulist," Cael said. Of that, he was certain. He'd held the real Devon Bradshaw in his arms.

He wanted to hold her right now.

"Don't worry, Cael," Tony said. He grabbed his brother's shoulder and gave it a squeeze. "We'll figure it out. Nothing's going to get your girl—not while we're on the job."

Everyone nodded in agreement, but Derek cleared his throat.

"That's all fine and good," he said slowly, "but there's one thing you haven't mentioned. Were you able to complete your rounds last night?"

Suddenly, the temperature in the restaurant seemed to drop ten degrees.

Shit. This was what Cael had dreaded about coming here today.

"I missed two of my charges," he confessed.

Shock froze the muscles in his brothers' faces. After what seemed like an eternity, Zane groaned and Tony let out a curse. Derek wiped a hand across his face. "This is bad, Cael. Really bad."

"You don't have to tell me." Dream Wreakers couldn't neglect their duties. Good dreams or bad, people didn't function well without them.

Tony let out a long breath. "You need to watch her, man. Watch her close."

Like he was capable of doing anything else.

"Maybe you should think about changing your plans," Derek said quietly. "Your daytime ones. If she recognizes you now . . ."

"No."

"But Cael, this changes everything."

"Exactly. After last night, I need to get as close to her as possible."

Derek leaned forward, impatience showing on his face. "You don't know what's motivating her or what her game is."

"And I need to figure it out. Did any of you stop to think that *she* might be the one in danger?" Cael's hands fisted, and he leveled an uncompromising glare at all of them. "Let's get one thing clear. Whatever happens, whatever needs to be done, *she's my problem.*"

Trouble or not, Devon Bradshaw was his.

Four

Cael watched as Devon fell asleep. She'd been resistant, but once she succumbed, she went down fast.

Or *did* she?

His senses reached out to test her. Until he knew for certain what had happened the other night, he had to be on guard against her. She was an unknown quantity, this woman he'd thought he'd known so well.

This beautiful seductress.

Unable to help himself, he let his gaze run over her. Her features were soft in sleep. Her lips were parted as if begging for a kiss, and her hair was spread across the pillow like a red waterfall. She looked harmless, almost vulnerable, and it made him ache.

If something had used her, or hurt her in any way . . .

"Hell to pay," he muttered, pushing the feelings down. He needed to concentrate. Regardless of the circumstances, she was still one of his charges. She needed to dream tonight.

She'd been avoiding him for too long.

He focused on his keener senses. Tonight, slumber had definitely taken her. Her theta waves were decreasing, and he could already feel the spindles starting to jump. Funny how the scientists had gotten that one right. They'd named the interesting brain wave phenomenon from what they'd seen on their EEG graphs, but spindles had a much more practical use for him. They were what he caught to pull a sleeper out of stage four and lead her into dreamland.

Which was exactly where Devon needed to go.

Cautiously, he moved toward the bed. For the past two nights, he hadn't been able to get near her. She'd been fighting her natural inclination to sleep. The other night had scared her, but avoiding rest was only making matters worse. He knew, because he'd ignored his own advice and had stayed with her, waiting for an opportunity to bestow a dream. By doing so, he'd neglected his other charges.

Again.

It was time for this to end. His questions were getting in the way of his normal routine. Tonight, he wasn't going to leave until he had some answers—and she had some relief.

Slowly, he reached for her. She shifted away.

His muscles tensed, ready for anything, but it was just the heat bothering her. He watched as she let out a groan and kicked at the covers. They tangled around her legs until she managed to break free. Almost at once, she settled back against the pillow.

Suddenly, Cael found it hard to breathe.

Trouble or not, she was still the most gorgeous thing he'd ever seen.

She'd bared her long, sleek legs, and his already alert cock stiffened. He knew now how those legs felt when they wrapped around his waist and held tight.

She was wearing another silky confection, one he liked a lot. Especially the slit. He went dead still when she rolled onto her side and drew up her knee for balance. That sexy slit was now exposing the tight curve of her bottom and a tiny slip of silk. Her panties.

His hands curled into fists. "Ah, Red."

He was supposed to get in here, do his job, and leave. Move on to the next charge and get caught up.

It just wasn't that easy. The pull he felt toward her was strong, nearly unbreakable.

Focusing on what he needed to do, he lifted his hand to her forehead. Brushing aside her hair, he settled his palm against her warm skin. Her body immediately went still, but her blood pressure and heart rate rose. He caught a passing spindle and led her into REM sleep—the sleep of dreams.

Automatically, he let himself slide into the dream with her. He'd never been able to avoid the temptation of hitchhiking along. It made him feel closer to her. Through her dreams, he'd come to know her. Her humor, her intelligence, her strengths, her flaws . . . But he hadn't foreseen her plans—if breaking through the dream barrier had *been* a plan. Tonight, this little joyride was all business. He needed to stay detached and read between the lines. If something was coming after his kind, he needed to know.

She'd barely gotten into the dream, though, when he felt her stir.

His brow furrowed. She wasn't supposed to be able to do that. People stayed absolutely motionless in the dream state, their muscles actually paralyzed. It was a protective mechanism that kept them from enacting the dream.

He concentrated harder, trying to follow along the wisps of her thoughts. They were elusive, almost as if she wasn't in REM. His gaze went to her eyelids. Her eyes weren't moving.

His hand jerked as he felt an unfamiliar pulse in her brain patterns. *What the hell was that?* Before he could identify it, her eyelids suddenly flew open. He pulled away from her sharply, but not before she looked up and saw him.

Truly saw him. Her green gaze was alert and fully conscious.

Cael froze. She'd done it again. Before he could figure out what to do, a slow smile curved her lips. His heart took off like a racehorse. How long had he wanted her to look at him that way? Her hands lifted, and she sighed in pleasure when her palms settled against his chest.

The touch put his dick in a full frenzy, and he couldn't pull away.

Devon smiled and relaxed when she saw the man looming over her. There he was—her own private, gorgeous hunk. All strong, dark, intense, and . . .

She suddenly remembered being caught against that muscled chest, trapped in an inescapable embrace. "You," she hissed as she scrambled away to the far side of the bed.

It was the wrong way to go. By moving away from him, she'd put something between them. Looking down, she saw an unwanted, familiar figure lying against her pillow. The sight immobilized her, turned her muscles to lead. "No," she whispered.

It was the same dream, only a different chapter.

She didn't want to go through this again. She forced herself to inhale deeply. Just as determinedly, she blew the air out through her mouth. The picture didn't improve.

No matter how hard she tried, she couldn't stop looking at the body—herself, her clone . . . *Whatever* that was on the bed beside her. Only . . .

"She's not dead."

For the first time since she'd exploded away from him, her dream man stirred. "No, I told you, she's you. Your other half. If you're okay, she's okay—and vice versa."

Devon glanced at him briefly, but as long as he remained on the other side of the bed, he was secondary in her concerns. She tried to look at the body detachedly. "She's . . . I'm breathing," she said.

Up close, she could see it in the moonlight.

Hesitantly, she reached out. Just as she was about to touch the body's shoulder, though, she lost her nerve. She snatched her hand back. "It's not good when you dream you're dead. At least, according to Freud." She forced a weak laugh. "I'm not sure what he'd have to say about this."

"Probably something lewd like you want to screw yourself."

Slowly, she looked toward her dream man. He met her look straight on, telling her they both knew that wasn't what she wanted at all.

His voice lowered. "When it comes to dreams, Freud was a hack."

A shiver ran through her. She'd been joking, trying to change the eerie nature of the game her mind was playing on her, but once again, she found she had no control here. Standing opposite the bed, her dream man looked powerful. All knowing.

It had been a mistake to dismiss him.

Moonlight poured through the window, giving the room an evocative glow. The shadows where the light couldn't reach were menacing, but he looked comfortable as they surrounded him. This nighttime world was his territory—and she'd invaded it.

He made a move toward her, and she instinctively pulled back. She'd been too trusting the last time. She didn't know the rules here, and she obviously didn't know him. She slid off the bed and put the wall at her back.

"Easy," he said, holding up his palms toward her. "I won't hurt you—either of you."

That was what he'd promised the last time, right before he'd swept her up toward terror. Devon's weight went to the balls of her feet when his fingers brushed against her sleeping form's temple. "Don't touch her!"

He hesitated. "Can you feel that?"

It was something she'd been wondering herself. She looked at him suspiciously, not knowing if she should answer truthfully. She did. "No."

He nodded. Still, when he gently settled his palm against her unconscious half's forehead, Devon's fight-or-flight instinct flared to life. Part of her wanted to push him away, to protect her sleeping twin. The other part of her wanted to run from the room. This dream was too much, too bizarre. She'd fought sleep in an attempt to avoid this. Sweat broke out on her brow as she stood there, torn but doing nothing.

"What is it?" she asked when his eyebrows drew together.

"Nothing," he said evasively. She watched as he swept a red curl onto the pillow. The action was tender, almost concerned. "Nothing's wrong; you're just sleeping."

And King Kong was just a gorilla. Devon swallowed hard. "So this is all just a dream?"

He wouldn't meet her eyes. "Yes."

"Like hell. This is a *nightmare*."

He looked at her, unfazed. Finally, he nodded. "You're right—and it's time for it to end."

Devon saw him flicker. Right before her eyes, he started to fade. It snapped her out of her inertia. "No!"

He wasn't going to leave her like this. His presence unsettled her, but not as much as being stuck divided in half. Not thinking, she lunged at him. Planting one knee on the bed, she leaned fearlessly over her sleeping body and latched onto his arm.

He faded until she could see right through him, but then he snapped back to full flesh and blood. The sudden change staggered him before he regained his balance. When he looked at her, his expression was stunned.

Devon pulled back slowly, hoping she hadn't just made things worse. He looked suspicious of her, wary. It scared her, and her heart began to thud. She wished desperately for herself to wake up.

It didn't happen.

She bolted toward the door instead.

Cael sprang into action. She wasn't going any-where—not until they figured this out.

He rounded the bed to head her off and caught her by the arm. She let out a cry. Whirling around, she clawed at him, but he pushed her up against the door, careful not to hurt her. Using his weight, he trapped her and pinned her wrists over her head.

She bucked against him, and his breath caught. She was tall enough to fit against him just where it counted most. His cock pressed right against the notch at the top of her legs. Those long, luscious legs . . . Her chest heaved and her nipples raked against his chest. He didn't need the reminder that only a thin layer of silk stood between them.

"Why am I dreaming these things?" she panted. She twisted her wrists in his grip. "Why can't I wake up?"

As much as he hated seeing her so upset, he couldn't let down his guard. She'd nearly dispersed with him! She would have traveled along wherever he'd gone.

"Tell me about the love spell," he said gruffly. "Whose idea was it? What made you do it?"

Her eyes narrowed. "*What made me do it?* What do you think?" She struggled again. "Seven months of feeling you watch over me. Seven months of sexual frustration! I did that spell to unstick my brain, but if this is the best alternative it can come up with, I must be going insane."

The hair on the back of Cael's neck stood on end, even as his balls drew up tight. Could it really be? As much as the idea turned him on, he couldn't believe a simple love spell could have that much power. Unless . . .

Her eyes widened when he caught both her wrists in one hand and reached for her forehead with the other. "What are you doing?"

"Hold still."

She jerked away, but he leaned more heavily against her, emphasizing the fit of their overheated bodies. She stilled, watching with trepidation as he pressed his palm against her forehead, flesh against hot flesh.

She trembled under his touch, but his sensitive nerve endings searched deeper. Normally he couldn't read a conscious person's mind, but she was an astral projection of a comatose sleeper and—

The truth hit him like a two-by-four.

She wasn't lying—she'd cast that spell on a lark. She truly believed this was all a flight of fantasy—*and her fantasy was him.*

Every muscle in Cael's body went rock hard. "Devon," he said in awe.

She tried to buck him off her again. "Let me go."

"Not on your life."

Her eyes became huge.

His heart was pounding and his thoughts were racing. "Am I your dream man, Sexy Red?"

The pulse at the base of her throat fluttered wildly, yet she looked at him as if he were an advancing tiger. "Not anymore."

He trailed his finger across her skin. "You're my fantasy woman."

She shivered but looked away. "Did I mention I think I'm going insane?"

"Doesn't matter. I'm crazy over you, too."

Slanting his mouth across hers, he kissed her. He kissed her like he'd always wanted, lips hard and tongue deep. She was potent. He let go of her wrists and fisted his hand into the lush thickness of her hair. His tongue swept deeper, searching for more sweetness.

He growled deep in his throat when he found it.

Devon froze, stunned by her dream man's lush kiss. She wasn't quite sure what was happening, why his mood had switched, but dreams were like that. Mercurial. Swift changing. She liked this side of him much better.

Hesitantly, she wrapped her arms around his neck and clung tight—until she remembered the last time they'd been in a clinch. "The bed," she said, tearing her lips away.

"Yes," he said, his eyelids heavy.

"No," she whispered. She gestured behind him. "I can't with that . . . with her . . ."

His dark eyes turned smoky, and his hands settled at her waist, nearly spanning it. Her breath caught when he slowly turned her around.

"Better?"

His heat and strength pressed against her back. The feeling was heady. Sumptuous. Reaching out, Devon braced her hands against the door. Her mind might be racing to catch up with the swiftly changing dream, but her body was having no trouble.

"I'm sorry if I scared you," he whispered into her ear. His cheek nuzzled against her hair as his arm stole around her waist. His fingers spread wide over her belly, and her hands unconsciously spread wider against the door.

His lips kissed a sensitive spot behind her ear, and her knees turned wobbly.

"Seven months of sexual frustration?" he asked softly.

The words seemed to pulse in the still night air. "Don't make fun of me."

He pressed his hips forward, and she felt his huge erection press into the cleavage of her butt.

"I'm not."

She shuddered when his hands moved. They slid under her nightie, lifting it as they stroked all the way up her body. He lifted the silk over her head and let it go. It fluttered downward, and his hand spread across her abdomen again before the garment could softly settle onto the floor.

The contact felt hot, possessive.

"You are so pretty in the moonlight," he whispered as he dipped his head. He placed soft kisses along her shoulder. "This skin—it glows."

He eased back and kissed the top vertebra of her spine. He gave the next one similar treatment and kept moving down until her bottom was clenching in anticipation.

He didn't even pause as he hooked his fingers in her bikini panties and kept on going.

"Dreamer," Devon breathed, bracing herself harder against the door.

She felt her panties slide down her legs and his mouth . . . It was gliding closer and closer to sensitive areas. She could feel him moving behind her. Crouching down. Settling in. Finally, he kissed her tailbone, his mouth right at the top of the crease of her ass.

He lingered there, his lips brushing her intimately.

Devon's pulse pounded in her ears. Things were spiraling out of control fast.

His fingers brushed against her inner ankles, her calves, her knees . . . She knew what he wanted. Up and down he stroked her thighs until she gradually widened her stance. Opening more . . . and a little more . . .

Finally, he reached his hand between her legs. Deep. All the way until his palm cupped the tidy patch of red hair that covered her mound and the tips of his fingers splayed across her pelvis. The embrace was hot. Explicit. With a gentle nudge of the base of his hand against her pubic bone, he tilted her hips back.

Devon's heart felt like it was ready for takeoff. Kneeling behind her, his intent was obvious. She sucked in heavy air . . . stared at the moonlight slashing across her hands against the door . . . listened to his steady breaths . . . As fast as her pulse was pounding and as hot as her belly was glowing, she could hardly believe this was a dream.

She felt his breaths, and all her senses zoomed in.

Then his mouth was on her.

"Ah!" she gasped, shocked at the intimacy. *Loving it.*

His fingers stretched against her belly, as his tongue stroked her down below. Like a starving man, he lapped at her pussy. He stroked over her peaks and dipped into her valleys.

"Oh, God!" Devon groaned when he ran the tip of that bold tongue around her sensitive opening. She let out a wild cry and her fingers threaded over his, gripping him tightly. He rewarded her by pushing his tongue into her and curling it.

"Ah! Oh! Yes."

He thrust in and out, and she began to come undone. Suddenly he changed tactics. Kissing down her slick labia, he found her clit. He wrapped his lips around it, and the pressure of his hand increased as he lifted her to his mouth and began to suck.

Devon's body fell forward against the door. Her thigh muscles clenched, and she began to shake.

She came hard, but it wasn't enough. Relentlessly, he used his tongue to bring her another wave of pleasure. At last, her body sagged, and he caught her to him as he stood up. Their damp skin clung as they leaned heavily against the door.

"You are incredible," he murmured into her ear. His hand brushed against the small of her back as he untied his pajama bottoms. She heard them fall to the floor. His feet planted inside hers, and she felt the big head of his cock find her slick notch.

She arched again when he thrust into her. Slowly. Deeply. Single-mindedly.

"God, Devon," he groaned.

His arm around her waist tightened. The other came up to cup a breast. Through it all, he kept his thrusts slow, sensuous. Devon threaded her fingers through his, reached back, and caught his hip. Her head rolled against his shoulder as he bent his knees and started driving up into her harder, faster.

"Dreamer!" she said, her voice going tight. Her body twisted in almost unbearable pleasure as he rammed into her, right to the hilt. His cock was big, and it was long. He was touching parts of her no other man had ever broached before, and the stretch felt incredible.

"So tight," he hissed as he held himself deep.

Devon's nipples pinched at the sensation. She'd

never felt anything like this. Her fingers bit into his hip. Over and over again, he thrust. Harder, then slower, then fast and deep.

She let out a cry when he settled in for a long grind. His cock was buried so deep in her pussy, she didn't know if he'd ever leave. He gave that extra little hitch of a thrust, and then he was spurting into her.

He let out a shout, and she climaxed right along with him. Her pussy squeezed at the sensation of his juices filling her, spilling onto her thighs. They clung to each other as pleasure rocked them both. Finally, they had to lean against the door for support.

Devon fought for air. Fought for consciousness.

"Mmmm," she hummed.

The energy just drained right out of her and she felt drowsy, replete.

Her dream man was fighting to stay on his feet, too. "Red? Are you okay?"

"So good," she murmured. Her eyelids were too heavy to keep open. They drooped until her lashes fanned against her cheekbones. Suddenly, her muscles released entirely. She felt him take her weight before she could fall to the floor.

"Devon?" he said sharply.

She was out.

And she was gone.

Fear and surprise ripped through Cael when he found himself standing alone. Devon's weight, the soft brush of her hair, and the silky cling of her skin—they all disappeared in a flash. Spinning around, he looked to the bed and rushed to her side. His hand shook as he reached out to her.

He nearly dropped to his knees when he found her whole again, sleeping peacefully.

With a groan, he sat on the bed beside her. Whatever she'd done to cross over the barrier, she hadn't been able to maintain the projection. He glanced down. Hell, he was surprised *he* had.

He fell backward onto the bed beside her.

Holy shit, that had been unbelievable.

Devon suddenly rolled toward him, and the way she cuddled against him left him flabbergasted. She couldn't see him now, couldn't possibly feel him—yet it was as if she knew he was there.

His arm went around her instinctively. "Baby, you are trouble."

Trouble that was worth it.

Cael was suddenly struck with a sense of responsibility so strong and pure, it nearly overwhelmed him. He had to protect her. She was too vulnerable. She didn't realize what she'd done. She didn't know the danger she posed, or the lines she'd crossed.

The dream realm was a dark, twisty place. For every bit of sensual delight that could be found in the shadows, peril threatened at every murky turn. The night was a sanctuary for lost souls, the outcasts. She didn't belong there.

Yet it felt so right having her at his side.

He wrapped a curl of her fiery hair around his finger. Something was definitely happening here—and he didn't just mean sex.

Slowly, he let out a long breath. As much as he wanted to stay, he knew it was time to go. There were others out there who needed him. He'd already stayed too long; there were charges that he'd never get to tonight.

Still, he had some answers.

Gently, he led Devon into REM sleep. Unable to leave without one last kiss, he brushed his lips across her forehead. "Sweet dreams, Sexy Red," he whispered.

Before he could give in to the temptation to stay, he got dressed, dispersed, and was gone.

Five

*B*ang!

The sudden noise made Tasha jackknife straight up in her bed. Her eyes flew open, and her heart nearly exploded from her chest. What the . . . ? Where . . . ? The sound had come from the wall. On her knees, she spun around, bracing herself for whatever was about to come through it.

All she heard from the other side was a muffled curse.

Dumbfounded, her jaw dropped. "Oh, you've got to be kidding me."

A wrecking ball hadn't hit. A bomb hadn't gone off. It was just Mr. Noisy, striking again. "That's it!" she growled.

Her neighbor had woken her up out of the soundest sleep she'd managed to get in days. Her gaze flew to the bright red digital numbers on the clock on her bedside stand. 6:08.

She hadn't fallen asleep until after four! Oh, this was war.

"Inconsiderate, self-centered *ass*!"

Late nights, she could understand. She was a night owl herself, but this new twit next door was going above and beyond. He partied every night, as far as she could tell, and he didn't get home until after the sun came up.

That would be fine with her if he would just keep *quiet*.

She unlocked her front door and whipped it open so fast, it thudded against the wall.

Good, see how he liked it.

Her bare feet slapped against the hallway floor as she marched to his door. Balling up her fist, she began to do some banging of her own. "Come out here, you noisy ox," she muttered underneath her breath. "I dare you."

She'd set up a rhythm that would have done Ringo Starr proud when the door suddenly flew open. Surprised, she stumbled forward a step but caught herself before she did a face-plant at her neighbor's feet.

"Do you *mind*?" she hissed.

"Keep your panties on," he grumbled.

"People are trying to sleep!" they said in unison.

Tasha finally looked up—and nearly swallowed her tongue. Holy cow! Mr. Blond, Toned, and Scrumpdil-lyicious looked right back at her.

He seemed to come up short, too.

"On second thought . . . ," he said, letting his gaze take a slow journey. It stuck on her boy shorts, and for a moment, he seemed to reconsider his request about her panties.

Tasha's thoughts scattered to the wind. She'd come over here for a reason, she knew. A good reason. What had it been?

God, who cared? The guy looked good enough to eat. He had that sandy hair that surfers got from spending hours in the sun, and his body . . . She nearly purred as she took in the physical perfection displayed before her. He was as tanned and honed as any beach bum she'd ever seen. She knew, because all he wore were white briefs.

Very brief white briefs.

He ran a hand through his rumpled hair. "Can I do something for you?"

Where should she even start? Heat unfurled deep in her belly at the sound of his low voice. Dragging her gaze away from his underwear, she looked up into his eyes. They were deep blue, but rimmed with fatigue.

Wait! That was it. She'd come over here because she was tired.

No, that didn't make sense.

"Do you need to borrow a cup of sugar?" Those deep blue eyes sparked. "Or maybe some clothes?"

He was laughing at her!

Self-consciously, Tasha pushed her hair over her shoulder. She must look like a maniac coming over here without even running a brush through her hair. Or putting on a robe! She suddenly realized she was nearly as naked as he was, but she was standing in the middle of the hallway where anyone could see. Her skimpy tank seemed to shrink as he stared.

He let out a disappointed sigh when she crossed her arms over her chest. "Honey, you look sweet, and damn if you haven't aroused my . . . curiosity . . . but I've had a long night. Is there a reason you were trying to put a hole in my door?"

The reason came back to her with startling clarity, and irritation hummed in her veins. Caustically, she lifted one eyebrow. "I thought it might match the one you were trying to put in my bedroom wall."

His brow furrowed in confusion, but then he glanced over his shoulder toward his bedroom. Understanding hit, and he let out a grunt. Turning back toward her, he leaned his forearm near her head, looking sheepish. "You must be the neighbor. Sorry about that."

Neither the apology nor the rippling of his chest muscles calmed her down. "*Sorry?* You've woken me every day since you moved in, and that's all you can say?"

He blinked, surprised by her outburst. "Um, I'm *really* sorry?"

"What was that noise?" she demanded, pointing to the bedroom.

He shifted uncomfortably. "My bed broke."

"Broke?" she sputtered. "Get serious."

"My buddies put it together when I moved in—or so I thought. They must not have tightened the screws."

Oh, she'd tighten the screws all right.

"Why don't I help you with that?" she said sweetly. With a quick duck, she slipped under his arm and marched right into his apartment.

He did a double take. "What the . . . ? Hey, wait a minute. What do you think you're doing?"

"If you want something done right, do it yourself," she threw over her shoulder.

Determined, she headed toward the bedroom. She knew exactly where it would be since his apartment was the mirror opposite of hers. Living room first, eat-in kitchen next. Boxes sat everywhere, still waiting to be unpacked. There weren't even chairs around the table yet. Men! She spied some tools on the kitchen counter and grabbed a screwdriver and some pliers as she made her way to the bedroom.

Sure enough, the bed was cockeyed and lopsided. The headboard was tilted and balanced precariously against the wall, right where her head had lain on the other side. No wonder it had sounded like a cannon being shot off.

"I am capable of fixing that," he said from the doorway.

"Yes, well I'm good with my hands."

His blue gaze sparked, then slowly ran down her form. "I bet you are."

Tasha let out a harrumph and grabbed the corner of the mattress. Oh, sure. Put a sexual spin on it while he stood there looking all hunky and she felt so bedraggled. With a surge, she tilted the mattress and pushed it off the disheveled bed.

"Hey!" His masculinity threatened, he came across the room. He jostled her accidentally and their butts bumped.

Tasha's eyes widened, and she scooted aside as he lifted the mattress as if it were a feather. He leaned it against the wall, and she rubbed her backside contemplatively.

"Don't even think about it," he said when he saw her eyeing the box spring. He quickly moved it out of the way, too.

Tasha felt herself weaken as she watched his muscles contract and release. The sight of the loose bed frame, though, put her right back into her bad mood. A monkey could put this thing together. For God's sake, it had wing nuts! His clumsy friends hadn't even managed to put the roller feet on correctly; one was missing entirely. She knelt down to put things right.

Unfortunately, he squatted down at the same time and their heads nearly knocked.

"Oh!" she said, her mouth a breath away from his. "Did I get you?"

His gaze fell to her lips. "Not yet."

Tasha's lips began to tingle so sharply she had to lick them. Damn, he was yummy. Out of the corner of her eye, she spotted the runaway wheel under the dresser. "Could you get that?"

He distractedly looked to where she pointed. When he stretched to pick the wheel up, he gave her a prime view of one grade-A backside. Her head tilted, and she nearly drooled.

When he turned back, she snapped upright. Focusing on the bed, she gave the wing nut on the support bar a solid turn. Maybe putting a peephole in the wall wasn't such a bad idea after all.

"You don't have to do this," he said.

"I'm up anyway."

He frowned as he reattached the wheel. "I said I was sorry."

The frame dropped back to the floor with a thunk, and Tasha rolled her eyes.

"Damn," he muttered.

She counted to ten. "If you could just be a little more quiet, I'd appreciate it."

"You're no quiet mouse yourself, you know."

She looked at him sharply.

"Do you really need to turn your stereo up to ten every time you play it?"

Her mouth rounded to a surprised O. He must be

talking about yesterday. She'd done some preliminary sketch work at home. "That was Aerosmith," she said, appropriately horrified. "And it was one o'clock in the afternoon!"

He stood and brushed his hands. "Prime sleep time for me."

Oh, he did *not* want to go there. "Maybe it's time you learned that you can't party every night."

"Excuse me?"

"Turnabout is fair play," she said simply. "You wake me up, I'll wake you up."

She stood and headed for the box spring. When she started to drag it to the bed, he caught her by the waist. "Baby, if you want to play, there are other, more pleasant games we could try."

Tasha's senses hummed, and she shifted her hips suggestively. "Is that an invitation?"

His fingers curled. "Absolutely."

She glanced over her shoulder. "Stop throwing those pots and pans around in the morning, and we'll talk."

Smoothly, she moved to the other end of the box spring.

His eyes narrowed, but he helped her pick it up and carry it to the frame. "If this is a negotiation, then you need to get rid of the high heels. They sound like a ball-peen hammer on your kitchen floor."

Tasha's spine stiffened. *Nobody* attacked her shoes. "It can't be any worse than the way you rap your razor against the edge of your bathroom sink when you shave. 'Rap, rap, rap.' Always three times. 'Rap, rap, rap' coming through the pipes. It drives me crazy!"

He laughed. "Try listening to your off-key singing in the shower."

She planted her hands on her hips. "I sing just fine! And besides, you slam doors."

His amused gaze slid down to her chest. "You vacuum too much."

Tasha glanced down. In her huff, her breasts were going up and down, her nipples jutting out like accusing fingers. She swiftly crossed her arms again. "Well, you . . . you . . ."

He held up his hands. "Truce. I'll concede that there's nothing either of us can do about the shoddy workmanship of this building." He walked back to get the mattress. "We'll just have to try to be more considerate."

Keeping one arm locked over her boobs, Tasha reached down with the other to help. The mattress tilted wildly, though, and knocked the bed stand against the wall.

She stared at the spot on the wall where it had hit. They'd have to walk around on tiptoes not to disturb each other.

It just wouldn't work! Even if it weren't impractical, she'd never remember to take off her shoes every time she went into the kitchen. And as for her music, she couldn't work without it. On top of everything else, now that she knew what he looked like, she'd listen to every little noise he made and try to imagine what he was doing. Sleeping, working out, showering . . .

Damn.

If only she could get some rest. She needed sleep so badly, she could cry.

Giving up on modesty, she reached down with both hands and helped lug the mattress to the bed. She dropped it down carelessly and straightened.

A wave of fatigue suddenly rolled over her. For a moment, her vision went dark and all she saw were stars. Blindly, she reached out for the wall, but she caught the unattached headboard instead. It slipped under her weight, and she started to go down.

"Whoa!" her neighbor said, moving fast. Somehow, he hooked an arm around her waist and kept her from hitting the floor. It knocked the wind out of her all the same.

Tasha fell against him, gasping for air. The stars behind her closed eyelids whirled. "Uh oh," she panted. "Major head rush."

"Shit." He cupped the back of her head and stopped her from standing all the way upright. "Take a moment. Breathe deeply."

"Try-ing."

"Try harder."

It took only a few seconds for the spell to pass. Or so Tasha thought. Everything was all right when she hesitantly straightened. When she tried to move away from him, though, her knees wobbled.

"That's it." Bending, he swung an arm under her knees and picked her up. "Hold on."

The world twirled just as she was beginning to see it again. She clamped a hand over her eyes, praying she wouldn't get sick. "Oh, God, don't do that. Put me down."

"I'm going to check you out first."

Why did guys always want to pick her up? She was tiny, but she wasn't feeble. "Put me down. I'm fi- What did you say?"

"Relax. I'm an EMT."

"A what?"

"Emergency medical technician. Sorry to burst your bubble, sweetie pie, but I'm not out partying at night. I work the graveyard shift."

Tasha went limp in his arms. Could this day get any worse? Six o'clock in the morning, and she'd already made a fool of herself. Not only did he work nights, he was a freaking hero.

Which meant the noise problem wasn't going to go away. His schedule ran directly opposite hers, and things weren't likely to change unless one of them moved. She was locked into her lease for another eight months.

"I will apologize for move-in day," he said, carrying her easily back to the kitchen. "I know we were noisy then. My coworkers came over after our shift to help me out. It was the only time we could all get together to do it."

"Oh, geesh. I never thought . . . I just assumed . . ." She sighed. "You must think I'm the biggest bitch, bursting into your apartment to rant like this."

The corners of his mouth twitched. "Honestly? I wasn't listening much. My brain kind of froze when I opened the front door and found you dressed like that."

He looked at her with such uncensored male appreciation, Tasha blushed. She couldn't believe it; she actually felt her face turn hot. She never got embarrassed anymore; she was the outrageous one, the bold flirt.

"I just . . . The bang against the wall . . ." She rubbed her hand nervously on her stomach and realized that her tank had hitched up. She felt the heat seep from her face down into her chest. "You have to understand, I've hardly slept in days. When you woke me again, I kind of snapped."

"Really? I hadn't noticed." He let out a chuckle. "Do you have a name, Whirlwind?"

She was embarrassed even to tell him. "Tasha St. James."

"Nice to meet you, Tasha. I'm Jason Rappaport." He looked around his kitchen, then set her on the table since there were no chairs. "Okay, now let's get serious. How's your head?"

"Fine. I just stood up too fast."

"Let me be the judge of that."

He moved in close and cupped her face in his

hands. Tasha inhaled sharply, but the once-over he gave her this time couldn't have been more clinical. It only made her feel worse.

"Has this light-headedness happened to you often?" he asked.

"No," she said grumpily. When a man looked deep into her eyes, she didn't want him to be analyzing the size of her pupils.

"Are you diabetic? Is your blood sugar low?"

"No." She pushed his touch away and scooted to the edge of the table. "Let me down."

He had fast hands; she had to give him that. They clapped over her hips to hold her in place.

"Not until I say so," he said firmly. "The truth now. How does your head feel? Any pain? Any lingering dizziness?"

"It aches," she admitted. "But just because I'm so tired."

Did he know where his hands were? Because she sure did. Her thin cotton panties might not have been there at all, as hot as his touch felt cupping her bottom.

"That might be the case, but humor me," he said. His grip tightened, and his thumbs slid into the creases at the top of her legs. "Think you can sit still for two seconds?"

Tasha felt her pussy clench. His thumbs were so close, it was taking everything she had not to rock back and forth on the table. If he wanted to touch her like that, they should go back to the bedroom. She'd show him how to break a bed the proper way.

"Stay put," he ordered, sliding those hot hands down her thighs. "I'll be right back."

Promise? she nearly called after him.

Her gaze clapped onto his backside as he walked away. Maybe letting him play doctor wasn't such a bad idea after all. She was all for medical experimentation if he could find a way to help her sleep.

Honestly, she was ready to try just about anything. Fatigue was hitting her like a two-ton hammer. She tossed and turned every night, then dragged the next day. Every time she tried to catch up with a nap, her eyelids popped open and refused to close. It was like her own body was fighting her.

Maybe she needed to try a new tactic—like a hot roll in the sack with her sexy new neighbor. If he wanted to use her in a test study, she'd be happy to volunteer.

She watched as he came back with a medical kit with a bold red cross on the side. The guy meant business.

"How long has it been since you got a full night's rest?" he asked as he set the kit down beside her.

Tasha peered into it with interest when he opened it. He had a stethoscope, gauze, and some liniment in there. Hmm. So many possibilities. "A week. Maybe more."

"Have you had problems like this before?"

"Not that have lasted this long."

"Has anything been bothering you?"

"Uh, you?" Feeling impish, she rubbed her toe against his shin.

He jerked, and the bulge behind his white briefs swelled. "I meant, are you stressed about anything?"

He didn't step away, so she swung her leg around his and delicately ran her foot up his calf. She loved it when his muscles jumped.

"I'm stressed about not sleeping." The less she slept, the more she worried about it. It was a never-ending cycle.

He let her curious foot wander. They both knew what she was doing, but he paid close attention as he wrapped a blood pressure cuff up her arm. "Have you changed your sleeping habits recently?"

"Ahem, *yeah*. That's the problem."

Tasha nearly moaned at the way his calf muscles pressed into her arch. She slid her foot higher and rubbed the back of his knee, trying to goad him into a response.

He grunted but covered it with a cough. He plugged the stethoscope into his ears and continued about his business. His face was serious as he pumped up the cuff and listened to her pulse. "Your blood pressure is a little high."

No kidding. She had a blond hottie standing so close, she could practically lick him.

"And so is your pulse," he said after a quick check.

Was that a hint of a smile she noticed?

He moved the cold stethoscope to her chest, but it was the proximity of his hand to her breasts that was making her nipples perk up so. The thin cotton tank hid nothing.

"Take a deep breath," he said.

The devil! She inhaled sharply and noticed his gaze became less professional and a lot more interested.

"Again," he ordered. "Slower."

Two could play at this game. She took a deep breath and held it. Feeling impish, she arched her back to give her breasts an extra lift. Pursing her lips, she let the air out, all the while looking into his blue eyes.

He hooked the stethoscope around his neck and leaned closer, settling his hands on the table on either side of her lap. "I'm not an expert, but I'd say you're suffering from insomnia."

Wrong. She was suffering from a bad case of horniness.

"What's the cause?" she murmured.

She knew the cause: the man was hot and she was bothered. She wanted nothing more than to wrap her arms and legs around him. He'd have her stripped and flat on her back in five seconds flat. Four, if the look in his eyes meant anything.

"It could be due to almost anything," he said. "The hot weather, a change in your diet—even the full moon tonight."

Her head came up slowly. "Full moon?" she whispered.

She looked into his blue eyes and almost melted. Oh God, could it be? Uncertain excitement suddenly made her nervous.

"There's no scientific proof, but people tend to act a little crazy around this time of the month." He shrugged. "I know things at work have been pretty wild. We've had more than the usual number of assaults and accidents. There were three car wrecks last night alone."

Tasha's mouth went dry, and she heard her pulse pound in her ears. "So something metaphysical could have brought me to your doorstep?"

"If that's what you want to call really good luck." He smiled, then got serious again. "You should go see your doctor."

Now, why did he have to go and say that? She cocked her head. "Can't you do anything to help me?"

His gaze dropped to her breasts and her nipples poked up so hard, they nearly popped through the fabric.

"I'd be more than happy to," he said, his voice going a little rough, "but I can't prescribe anything for you."

Her thrill dampened. "You think I need a *prescription*?"

"You've been without sleep for too long." Gently, he ran his finger along the dark circles under her eyes. "There are some good hypnotic drugs on the market. You could take them for a week or two until your circadian rhythm returns to normal."

Tasha went very still. She was ready to try just about anything—except that. "I'm more of a homeopathic sort of girl. Aren't there some home remedies I could try?"

"Sure. Try to make things in your bedroom as soothing as possible."

"No exploding walls?"

His eyes narrowed, but he let the shot pass. "Go to bed at the same time every night. Exercise, but not too late in the day. Watch your caffeine intake."

"I've done all of that."

"Then you should take something."

It was amazing how five little words could crush the light inside her so quickly. The spell was supposed to bring her Mr. Right. Either fate had a bad sense of humor or she'd jumped to the wrong conclusion entirely. She looked at him, so muscle-bound and gorgeous. She really didn't want to be wrong.

But he had knocked Aerosmith. And his schedule wasn't conducive to hers. Maybe he wasn't The One.

She had to give it one more shot. "Vanilla or chocolate?"

He hesitated. "Excuse me?"

"What do you like best? Vanilla or chocolate?"

"I don't know . . . vanilla?"

Her shoulders slumped. Spell, schmell. She needed to keep looking.

"What does that have to do with anything?" he asked.

"Never mind. My brain is just foggy."

Lines of concern appeared on his forehead. "Let me recommend somebody for you."

She shook her head and slid off the table. It put her right into his arms. He was warm and solid and the perfect fit for her. Not too tall; just right. Too bad the idea of a no-strings fling didn't appeal to her anymore.

"You seem like a nice guy. If we'd met under better circumstances, I'd probably be licking Hershey's syrup off of you by now." She ran a hand across his chest, then stepped around him, heading to the door. "As it is, my head hurts and I'm cranky. If you could just try to be quieter so I can get some rest, I'd appreciate it."

He nearly dropped his stethoscope. "Hershey's syrup?"

Damn, had she said that out loud? She backed out of the kitchen. "I just need to find a way to relax and I'll be all right."

He took a step toward her, the bulge in his shorts so heavy it strained the fabric. "We could try the Hershey's thing."

She smiled ruefully. "I need to go."

He reached out and caught her hand. "Hold on. At least let me give you some aspirin for your headache."

Her last hope for a little bit of magic died.

"Go to bed, Jason. I'll be quiet, I promise." She shook her head in resignation. "One of us around here needs to sleep."

Six

Dusk was waning and night was settling over the city when Devon finally made it to Tasha's studio. Wanting to get inside, she hurried down the empty sidewalk to the shop's door. The Solstice Arts District was just east of downtown, approaching the industrial zone. Although the area was in the midst of a revitalization effort, it was a bad part of town to wander at night.

She welcomed the blaze of light pouring out of Tasha's shop. She knocked but found the door unlocked.

"Tasha," she called as she stepped inside. "I'm here. Sorry I'm late."

"Well, it's about time," a disembodied voice answered from the back work area. "Where have you been?"

"Working."

"Is there a problem with your cell phone?"

Devon set down the takeout she'd grabbed at Chen Go's. Apparently she wasn't the only one who'd had a long day. "I was on assignment at the Equinox Bridge; there was a jumper."

Tasha's face popped into the doorway. "Was anyone hurt?"

"The police negotiator talked him down." Devon frowned. "Are you feeling okay?"

Tasha ran a hand over her face. "Sorry. I'm hungry, and I'm cranky."

And tired. Devon could see the fatigue in her friend's normally bright eyes. She pointed to the bag of food. "I brought Mongolian beef."

Tasha trudged into the front room, causing Devon to do a double take. Quickly, she moved to pull the shades over the windows. "Tasha! Where are your clothes?"

Her friend looked down and shrugged carelessly. She didn't seem to mind that she wasn't wearing anything under her painter's smock. "It got hot in here today. I fired up the kiln."

"Lock the door next time!" Devon said, moving to do just that. "What were you thinking?"

"I'm working on a new piece . . ."

Tasha glanced pensively toward her work area, and Devon felt pinpricks on her skin. Something was off. Usually her friend was excited and happy when she started a new project.

Watching her cautiously, Devon moved to the computer behind the front desk. She had to send her photos in before the print deadline.

Tasha opened the bag of food. Wonderful scents rolled out, but she scowled. Apparently not as hungry as she claimed, she picked out an egg roll and glanced back again to her work area. Devon's hands paused as she removed her camera from around her neck.

"You're still not sleeping well," she declared.

"No," Tasha said absently. Acting as if Devon weren't even there, she headed back to whatever had captured her imagination.

Devon was torn as she watched her friend disappear. She looked back to the computer screen. "Damn."

One thing at a time.

Trying to concentrate, she uploaded the photographs from her Canon EOS Digital Rebel. She braced herself as the pictures came onto the monitor. Tonight it had been a jumper. Earlier it had been a fire at Copyworks down on Constellation Street. The strife was getting to her. For days, she'd been running from one accident or fight scene to the next. Most mornings, she didn't even want to get out of bed. She just wanted to keep sleeping.

And dreaming.

She glanced at the clock. Bedtime wasn't that far away—but her deadline was sooner.

Distancing herself, she looked over the shots she'd

taken. She knew what Tommy expected; more importantly, she knew what he wanted. She shook her head.
It was a terrible time for her editor to leave. Solstice
seemed to be in full meltdown, and everyone at the
Sentinel was working overtime. It was a difficult situation for someone new to step into. Everyone was nervous about the upcoming changeover.

Right now, though, she was more nervous about
her best friend. She e-mailed the best of the shots to
the newspaper and went to the back room.

She hesitated when she found Tasha slowly circling
a clay model—one she didn't like at all. "Is that it?"

"Yes."

The maquette was Tasha's starting point for her
new sculpture, but Devon felt cold just looking at the
piece. When a pang hit her in the belly, she knew her
instincts were right on.

She glanced at Tasha. Her friend was looking upon
the sculpture with an oddly revolted yet entranced
expression on her face. "Were you commissioned to
do this?" Devon asked.

"No, it just came to me."

"It's very . . . dark."

"It's how I feel."

Devon stopped at her friend's side, tension radiating through her. Tasha was an unusually successful
artist, but her work was upbeat and joyful. This preliminary clay sculpture was completely opposite and
unlike anything she'd done before. It showed a wraith-

like figure writhing up from the ground. It was formless and faceless, haunting and moody. The dark clay only made it worse.

"Tasha," Devon said worriedly.

"I need to get it out," Tasha whispered, almost as if she didn't want to speak out loud in front of the thing. She looked at Devon as if confessing to something terrible. "I'm more than tired; I feel like my emotions are out of control. They're riding right at the surface. I have no on/off switch, no mute button. I know I was bitchy to you just now, but I can't stop it."

"That's all right; it's the insomnia. Honey, you need to go to the doctor."

"You and Jason!"

Devon paused. "Who's Jason?"

Tasha finally seemed to focus. Surprisingly, she even blushed. "My neighbor, the EMT."

Devon looked into her friend's eyes and suddenly felt heat. It banged into the middle of her chest, nearly sending her reeling. Her breath caught, but just as her heart was beginning to jump, it was gone. The effect was dizzying.

"Is this Mr. Noisy?"

Tasha shrugged. "It's not intentional; he works nights. He's not that bad."

Devon pressed her fingers against her temple. She'd experienced good impressions before, but nothing like that.

Tasha liked this guy. *Really* liked him. She was going to have to check him out.

"So he thinks you should see a doctor, too?" Devon asked, broaching the subject carefully.

Tasha's chin set. "Just leave it alone, would you?"

"No, this isn't like you. You've never had a sleeping problem before, and it's affecting your whole personality." Devon pointed at the model. "Look at that! It worries the hell out of me."

"But Jason said the doctor would put me on *sleeping pills*. You know I can't do that!"

Tasha had an extreme distrust of doctors and their prescription pads. As a teenager she'd experienced a serious injury, and painkillers had become too close a friend.

"I'm sure things have changed. The doctors will be more careful. *You'll* be more careful."

"I'm not sure I will—not with the way I feel." Tasha's shoulders slumped, and she rubbed the balls of her hands against her eyes. "What did I do to deserve this? Why can't I just sleep?"

Devon glanced to the back window of the studio and went still. Outside she could see the moon low on the horizon, big and full of secrets.

The waxing moon hadn't passed.

Oh, God.

"What?" Tasha said, catching her expression.

"It just occurred to me that since we did that

spell, your sleep problems have gotten worse. Mine have . . . improved."

"Is *he* still visiting you?"

Devon couldn't meet her friend's fierce gaze. Tasha considered her dream man the boogey man, something to be feared.

Devon didn't fear him at all, not anymore. He came to her every night, and her new dreams were so vivid and erotic, she never wanted them to end. She felt safe with him, cared for. It was much better than what she saw happening in the daytime world.

"When was the last time you slept well?" she asked, evading the subject. "When did you feel like you got recuperative rest?"

Frustration and suspicion darkened Tasha's face.

"If you won't take sleeping pills, we have to find another solution!"

They faced each other in a tense standoff until Tasha raked a hand through her hair. "I slept well on your couch. It was for too short a time, but at least I felt better when I woke up."

"Then come stay at my place. You can sleep in the guest bedroom. You know you're welcome anytime."

Tasha shook her head, and her gaze went back to the clay model. She looked almost obsessed. "Not tonight. I want to work on this some more."

The herbalist's words suddenly echoed in Devon's head. *Take the utmost care.* He'd been worried about the spell's unwanted side effects.

She looked at Tasha, feeling uneasy.

God, she hoped that wasn't what this was.

It was still early when Tasha walked tiredly across the lobby of her apartment building to the elevator. After Devon had left, she hadn't made it fifteen minutes longer at her studio. She'd just run out of steam.

But she felt better.

She didn't think her friend got that.

Working on the maquette helped. She was a visual person. It helped to look at things. It helped to deal with them. She felt lighter, happier—which was how she preferred to spend her life. She'd felt the darker side once, and she didn't want to go back there. Why waste time like that?

She punched the up arrow, and the doors opened. Stepping inside the world's slowest elevator, she hit the button for the sixth floor and settled into the corner. Wrapping her hands around the railings, she let out a yawn.

Yes, she felt more content. Controlled.

Sleepy.

The elevator started moving up, the motion smooth and lulling. For just a moment, Tasha closed her eyes . . .

She heard a ding just as she started dreaming the most lovely dream.

"Mmm," she hummed. Strong hands had wrapped around her waist. The feeling was protective. Sexy.

She slid her palms up a well-built chest and peeked between her eyelids. Jason.

"Hi," he said, looking at her bemusedly.

"Hi," she said, smiling back at him. Yum, elevator sex.

Sweet dream.

Wrapping her arms around his neck, she pulled him down for a kiss. His eyes widened, but he didn't resist. His blond head came down, and his lips sealed hard across hers.

Tasha rubbed herself against him. Oh, God. He knew how to use those lips. Her fingers threaded through his soft hair, and her tongue darted into his mouth. His groan went right through her.

"Whirlwind," he said, pulling back.

She slid her leg between his and pressed lightly. The blue in his eyes darkened.

"If you insist." His mouth came back to hers fast, and the hands at her waist glided down to her hips. He pulled her tighter against him and rubbed his growing erection against her intimately placed thigh.

Tasha felt light, floating. He pressed her back harder into the corner, and she giggled. This was the best she'd felt in a week. Working her arms around him, she grabbed his butt.

He jerked just as the elevator bell dinged.

"Oh, my!" said a surprised female voice.

Jason suddenly pulled back, and Tasha frowned.

"Don't mind me. I can wait for the next one."

"Come in, Mrs. Howell." His voice sounded rough, and red color burned up his neck.

Tasha couldn't make sense of things. She wasn't ready for this part of the dream to end. She let go of his firm butt with one hand and flicked her wrist at their elderly neighbor. "Shoo."

"Tasha," he said firmly. Reaching down, he detached her other hand from his posterior. "Wake up."

"Oh, for God's sake. Go to sleep. Wake up. Make up your mind."

A grin pulled at his lips again. "This isn't a dream."

She looked at him, confused.

"You fell asleep standing up. I found you when I got on the elevator."

She looked around. She was in the corner where she'd propped herself up. He was dressed in his EMT uniform, ready for work. She watched Mrs. Howell step hesitantly inside the elevator. "What are you doing here?"

If she was inviting Mrs. Howell into her erotic dreams, something was twisted.

Her neighbor blinked at the blunt question. "I'm just getting home from bingo."

Reaching out, Jason hit the button for the sixth floor. "It's getting worse, isn't it?"

Tasha watched him mutely. She'd thought it had just gotten a whole lot better.

His hand cupped her face, and his thumb

skimmed along her cheekbone. "Come down to the hospital with me. I talked with one of the doctors about your sleep problems. Let's get you something to fix this."

Something to fix this. Oh, she'd heard that one before. Settling her hands against his navy blue T-shirt, she pushed him away. He didn't want to go, but he stepped back as the elevator arrived once again at their floor. Watching them wide-eyed, Mrs. Howell stepped out into the hallway.

"This is where I get off, too," Tasha said.

For a moment, she thought Jason might block her way. He let her pass, but his face was set with concern. She let her gaze drop lower just before the doors closed. His cock was even harder.

Heat flared in her cheeks as she turned to find Mrs. Howell watching shamelessly.

"Oh, don't worry, dear," the older woman said kindly. She wrapped an arm around her shoulders. "If I were thirty years younger, I'd be bussing him in the elevator, too. He reminds me of my Harold, rest his soul—all sexy and spectacular."

Tasha's eyes flew open.

"I'm not blind, dear."

Tasha wasn't blind, either—or immune. Her motor had just been jump-started, and now there was no place to go. She looked down the hallway toward their apartment doors.

"Well, damn." She knew she'd get no sleep now.

Her adrenaline was pumping, her skin felt sensitive, and lust was roaring inside.

She hadn't worked that one into her clay model.

But it was there, and it was insistent. She felt warm all over and excited. He'd kissed her, and she'd nearly climbed him like a tree. Her nipples felt hard, and her pussy felt soft.

They came up to her apartment door, but she just stared at it. She didn't want to lie down on her bed. She didn't want to squirm until she heard him come home.

She needed to sleep. Why, she could have made out with Enos, the night watchman! Ew!

"Mrs. Howell?"

"Yes, dear?"

"Will you please take me to Devon's?"

Cael tried to make himself stay away. For nights now, he'd been falling asleep and transporting straight to Devon's bed. It was as if he had no choice; he had to see her.

When they were together, the outside world disappeared. He was finally able to touch her like he'd always wanted, stroke her soft skin, luxuriate in her silky hair. And she wanted him as badly as he wanted her. He heard it in her sighs every time he kissed her red lips or licked her tight nipples.

Even now, he felt the need to go to her. It was pulling at him, driving him crazy, but he needed to do his job. She'd kept him away from his duties for too long.

He concentrated on his sixth sense, scanning the airwaves for sleepers. Already, the nocturnal world was coming alive. He could sense the night, feel what was happening in all the dark, hushed corners. What he discerned, though, put him on edge. There were too many out there who needed his care. Too many whom he'd ignored since he'd become entangled with the beautiful redhead. He could feel their suffering; it buffeted him. His charges needed the relief only he could provide.

His focus sharpened. There was no excuse for his neglect, and the effects were already starting to show. Tonight, he couldn't be distracted. Too many people depended upon him.

Including one of his charges, who he suddenly sensed in Devon's house.

"What the hell?" His spirit skidded to a stop as it traversed silently through space.

Somebody else was sleeping in that house.

Jealousy tore through Cael. He knew it was unwarranted. He had no claim on her. Hell, she thought he was a frickin' dream. But so help him, if another man was touching her . . .

His senses honed in like a laser beam, but he couldn't identify the presence. The brain waves were sluggish, almost chaotic, but there was something familiar about the energy.

His jealousy vanished as quickly as it had come. He knew who it was, and it wasn't some other man.

It was Tasha—his spunky little Tasha.

A sense of urgency welled up within him. Normally he could sense her distinctive wave pattern anywhere. She depended heavily on the right side of her brain, the center of creativity, but things were no longer balanced. Her artistic hub was overstimulated, overloading from the lack of dreams.

She needed him *badly*.

He'd missed her too many nights in a row; he had to get down there and help her.

Everything inside him made him want to hurry, but he manifested in the living room of the old home carefully, scanning brain activity as he went. He couldn't run into Devon. Not now. The house was silent, except for the normal creaks and groans of hundred-year-old construction. His senses quickly found his redhead. She was upstairs, just slipping into the hypnagogic state—that hazy no-man's-land between wakefulness and true sleep.

His tense muscles relaxed. She wouldn't be able to sense him like that.

His attention turned to the dark-haired beauty on the sofa.

Tasha looked so small and vulnerable in the hazy light of the full moon. Even in sleep, she looked exhausted. The circles under her eyes were his fault, proof that she'd needed him and he hadn't been there.

Softly, he brushed her hair away from her face. "I'm sorry, pet," he whispered.

She was one of his favorites—so lively and animated. It was amazing how so much energy could be bound up in such a little package. Her dreams were so complex and intricate. Creative types like her needed his healing touch more than others. Without the outlet of dreams, her imagination could overwhelm her.

And he'd abandoned her.

"I'm here now," he whispered. He'd take the pain away.

He settled his hand over her forehead and closed his eyes. Immediately he sensed slow, large delta waves. She was in the deepest stage of sleep, stage four. It was recuperative for her body, but not what she needed most. He searched for the spindles that would guide her back up to REM.

They were hard to catch.

It took him three tries before he connected with one of the disjointed, sharp jumps. Almost at once, her blood pressure and pulse rate started to rise. Good, she wasn't going to fight him on this. He'd just begun to help her slide into a dream when he felt a disturbance.

His guard went up. There was another presence in the room.

Lunatics!

Cael's blood ran cold. The full moon was a day away, and they were on the prowl. Spinning around, he placed himself in front of his charge to protect her. Tasha was at her most vulnerable at this crossover stage. He couldn't let them take her over the edge into Lunacy.

Surprise made his muscles tighten.

"Devon," he whispered.

She stood at the base of the stairs, looking at him standing over her friend. Confusion wracked her face. She looked ethereal in the moonlight. An enchantress with hair of flames and eyes of emerald.

He fought the attraction that pulled him toward her. This was new, and it wasn't good. She'd crossed into the dream realm even though he hadn't been with her.

She shouldn't be here. She shouldn't be able to seek him out like this.

"Go back upstairs," he said softly. He needed time to figure out this new twist and tend to Tasha. "I'll be there in a minute."

Her green eyes flicked toward him. They were full of pain—and jealousy. "What are you doing? You're not Tasha's heart's desire," she said flatly. "You're *mine*."

Seven

Tasha's heart's desire?

Cael went still. What did that mean? Nobody talked that way, certainly not Devon.

"Did we get it that wrong?" she asked. Obviously upset, she ran a hand through her hair. With each glance between him and her friend on the couch, the hurt in her green eyes grew.

"Get what wrong?" he asked carefully.

"Were we not supposed to say it at the same time? Did the . . . I don't know . . . the signals get crossed somehow?"

She wasn't making sense, but with each word, his feeling of foreboding grew. Something was wrong here. Very wrong. As much as he hated to leave Tasha without taking care of her, he slowly headed toward Devon. "What signals, Red? What are you talking about?"

"The spell! I thought it might have backfired, but not like *this*."

Uneasiness pricked at Cael. Reaching out, he caught her by the chin and made her focus on him. "Backfired how?"

"Are you *her* dream man, too?"

The question threw him. "Tasha did the spell?"

"It was her idea."

He should have known. He knew how the imp's mind worked; he was her dream man—just not the way Devon suspected.

Yet as he watched his redhead carefully, he caught the jealous look in her eyes. It made his balls draw up tight. Stepping forward, he crowded her. He wanted no misconceptions about this. "Red, I'm all yours."

She inhaled deeply, and her breasts brushed against his chest. Still, she reached out and caught him possessively by the waist. "With the way you were standing over her . . ."

"I was looking for you," he lied.

Her touch went right through him, emphasizing just how susceptible he was to her. Her sensuality drew him in, captured him.

A niggling thought occurred to him. The pull was almost *too* powerful. "Devon, what exactly was that spell supposed to do?"

"Lead us to Mr. Right."

It was all he could do not to take her down to the floor. "But Tasha hasn't found hers yet?"

Devon looked uncomfortable. "I know you're just a dream, but she was serious about the whole thing."

Just a dream—he was so goddamned frustrated with that!

Reining himself in, Cael glanced to the sofa. He needed to concentrate on his charge; she was supposed to be the reason he was here. "How's she been feeling?"

"Moody and unsettled. Ever since we cast the spell, she hasn't been able to sleep."

More importantly, she hadn't been able to *dream*. That was his fault.

Devon shook her head slowly. "I thought this Jason guy might be the one for her, but what if she can't sleep because she's still searching? The full moon is tomorrow. What happens if she doesn't find anybody?"

Warning signs flared in Cael's head. He thought he knew what Tasha's problem was, but magic was an uncertain thing. "Tell me the spell, Devon."

She blushed. "I didn't believe it would actually work."

"But it did." Big time. "Humor me."

Her green gaze met his. Yet when her lips finally started to move, her voice was at a mere whisper. "Earth, Water, Wind, and Fire, lead me to my heart's desire. Bring passion, love, and romance before the waxing moon has passed."

The words were so simple, yet so powerful. They hit Cael square in the chest, and his heart began to pound. He looked at Devon standing in the moonlight; so beautiful, so guileless.

It had been as easy as that. He was her dream man, the one *she'd* chosen.

His hand shook as he caught her by the nape of the neck. "Come here," he said gruffly.

They moved as one, and the kiss was hot and wet, hard and deep. Her body fell against his, all lean lines and supple curves. Cael slid his tongue into her mouth, and the contact made him groan.

Unable to get enough of her, he kissed her cheek and the velvety lobe of her ear. "Passion, love, and romance?"

She arched her neck. "I thought about you when I said it. I pictured you watching over me in my dreams."

He couldn't remember the last time he'd gotten so hard so fast.

"This isn't a dream, Sexy Red. This is as real as it gets."

Reaching under her nightie, he slid his hand between her legs. She gasped in surprise, and he cupped her heat intimately.

"I've wanted you for the past seven months, too."

Looking into her eyes, he pushed the crotch of the flimsy panties to the side and slid two fingers into her. She let out a long groan that he caught with another kiss.

"I'll take care of Tasha," he said against her lips. "Don't worry about her."

She shuddered. He knew she was confused at what was happening. He wasn't sure what was going on either, but she could be certain about this. He wanted her, and he'd watch over her. Astral projection or full-flesh woman—he'd take her any way he could get her.

Increasing the pressure, he worked his fingers higher into her pussy. She was red hot to the touch. And tight. So unbelievably tight.

She caught his wrist. "We need to go somewhere else."

He looked to the couch. Tasha would never hear them. She'd never be able to see them. Still, Devon was right. They needed their privacy.

Determinedly, Cael directed them toward the kitchen.

Devon inhaled sharply when he didn't remove his hand. Watching her response closely, he stroked her until his fingers were in to the hilt. The intimacy made her even wetter, and her juices spilled onto her thighs as she followed him.

Cael couldn't believe how turned-on he was. Rolling into the kitchen, he braced his back against the wall.

It was the only thing that kept him on his feet when the power hit him dead-on.

He was caught unaware. Unprepared. He fought

just to breathe. Instinct told him to disperse, but he couldn't. The sensation that had captured him was so strong, it nearly smothered him. Holding on to Devon tightly, he scanned the room for the source. But that was just it—it was the room. It was an energy center. Currents flowed and shifted around them so rapidly, it made his senses swirl.

"Is this where you performed the ceremony?" he asked.

"Yes. At the stove."

Where heat was radiating like a blast furnace.

Cael's attention slowly swung back to the woman in his arms. A power vortex like this didn't occur by accident. It may have been a simple little spell, but that wasn't where the power had lain. It was within her!

"Devon," he said, stunned.

He understood now why he never wanted to leave her, why it was so hard to stay away from her. This was no ordinary spell. She'd put all her needs and desires into it, causing him to neglect his other charges. Somehow, her love spell had not only led her to him; it had bound him to her in return.

But not unwillingly.

He kissed her hard, and the power built. The force was undeniable. It tied them together, and Cael felt his own powers surge.

His thumb swept over her pussy, looking for her clit. She went up on tiptoe when he found it.

"Ah!" she cried. He settled the pad of his thumb over the bud. He stroked it, and she bucked.

He knew he was pushing her fast and hard. He couldn't help it. The magic between them was strong. She'd crossed into an entirely different realm to get to him.

Tearing his mouth away from hers, he bent her backward over his supporting arm. The tendrils of her hair looked like upside-down flames as they swung and danced. The position made her breasts thrust upward, and he greedily latched on to the nearest nipple through the silk.

Her body convulsed and she let out a cry as her hands raked down his back.

"More," he demanded. His nerve endings were firing. The power around them was rising and falling, reaching higher peaks with every swell.

Opening his mouth wide, he suckled her. The fabric became sodden as he worked her nipple with his tongue, his teeth, his lips . . .

"Dreamer," she gasped.

He pumped his fingers in her soft pussy, the sound wet and hot. She whimpered, ready to slam headfirst into an orgasm.

He eased a third finger into her, nudged her nub with his thumb, and she went off like a firecracker.

The air around them crackled as static electricity let loose, and Devon shook for what seemed like minutes as Cael held on to her, leading her through. His fingers rode her hard and his teeth toyed with her nipple until all her energy was drained. When her body finally sagged, he picked her up.

"My turn," he growled. He laid her on the kitchen table but felt his heart clench as he looked down at her.

Love spell or not, she wasn't meant for his world. It was too dangerous. Just look at the power flaring around them. He couldn't keep her safe here. Maybe back on the corporeal plane . . .

He caught her by the backs of her thighs and pushed them to her chest. Her panties were still hooked to the side of her wet pussy, exposing her to the moonlight coming through the kitchen window.

He took a ragged breath. "The heart's desire," he whispered in wonder.

Slowly, he ran his index finger down her swollen slit. She was plump and slick, and the mystical vortex in the room roared back to life.

"One last time," he said fiercely. One last time, he'd give in.

Then, this spell needed to be broken.

Devon felt drained, but the energy in the room was starting to fill her all over again. It started in the middle of her chest, around her heart, and spread outward to her extremities. Soon, her entire body was abuzz.

Lifting her heavy eyelids, she looked up at her dream man. Moonlight silhouetted him from behind, outlining his masculine form. He looked like a Greek god as he stood over her, his body chiseled as if from stone. His shoulders were wide, and his chest was deep. His waist was rippling with muscles, and down below . . .

She watched as he stripped and then his hungry cock was there, standing almost straight up in the hazy blue-white light. He was getting ready to take her up that hill again.

That crazy, frightening, earth-shattering hill.

In the shadows she couldn't see his expression, but he seemed almost possessed as he looked down at her. She felt the same way. He was hers, *her* heart's desire. The link she felt between them was indestructible.

"Dreamer," she sighed.

With her panties stretched the way they were, she knew he could see right down to the very heart of her. His fingers slid down her slit, opening her as he went, and her pussy fluttered. A grunt left his throat.

The sound was so sexy, Devon squirmed on the table. He stopped her by quickly clamping down on her hips. It emphasized the position he'd trapped her in, knees pulled to her chest, pussy lifted. Heat filled her entire body, but being so exposed and open was somehow freeing.

"Take me," she whispered.

Power crackled in all four corners of the room.

He spread her legs wider so her knees bumped against the outside of her breasts, framing them. "No, Sexy Red. You take *me*."

He grabbed her panties and pulled them down. They stretched thin, pulling taut around her thighs.

Devon clutched the edges of the table, her fingers turning white as she held on tight. Already, the room was starting to twirl.

"Hurry," she begged.

He pulled her hips down to the very end of the table, and excitement bubbled inside her chest. She was so wet, if he didn't do something soon—

"Ah!" she cried as he thrust into her, going all the way to the hilt. Her bottom pressed hard into the table beneath her. He leaned into her heavily, using his weight to go extra deep. Her cry intensified and she felt her cunny spasm about him, clamping down hard.

"Oh, God," he groaned.

Pulling back, he nearly left her. Devon rolled her hips upward, trying to hold on to him. He thrust forward again, deeper.

The table knocked against the wall, and her palms got slippery as she tried to hold on. "Ohhhh," she moaned.

The pleasure was so dark and sharp.

"That's good," he hissed. "Just like that."

His hands locked on to the backs of her thighs, holding her open. He plunged and withdrew, only to come back and grind against her again. Devon squirmed in delight. His cock was hot and big. It filled her until she couldn't want any more.

Much too soon, she felt herself start spiraling upward. She opened her eyes and, to her astonishment, saw colors dancing around him.

They were the same colors she'd seen dancing on the walls when she'd cast the spell!

She arched against the table as a swirling gust filled the room.

"Yes!" she cried. Her body felt as if it were ready to take flight. Power filled her, filled him, consuming them both.

"Devon," he gasped.

Her hands clapped onto his wrists, and she lifted her hips to meet his thrusts. Their bodies slapped together more urgently as the wind whipped and the colors burst. The cacophony was deafening, rising in strength, until a clap of thunder rent the room.

Her climax was so fierce, it felt as if a white light exploded inside her. Her dream man went rigid, and their bodies locked together as the power surged. She clung to the energy coursing through her veins, but it was like trying to hold on to a shooting star.

The energy slipped from her grip, and she sagged back onto the table.

He came right with her, leaning heavily onto her as their harsh breaths mingled in the moonlight. Tiredly, Devon lifted her arms and wrapped them about him to keep him close.

"Holy shit," her lover said hoarsely. "What have you done to me?"

She spread her fingers wide, luxuriating in his strength. "I think you did it to me."

He lifted his head, and she felt his dark stare again. It made her go all shivery inside. God, she loved his eyes. She'd always loved them.

Gently, he brushed her hair off her face. "So innocent, yet so dangerous," he said in awe.

She'd never been called dangerous before. She rather liked it.

But he was the one who was truly dangerous, lurking in shadows, haunting her dreams. "I wish you were real," she whispered impulsively.

She felt him tense. "And if I were?"

She brushed her fingers down his strong jawline. He was too perfect to be real. "Not even I could dream that."

His head dipped, and he went quiet.

Too quiet. Devon ran her fingers soothingly through his hair. "What's wrong?" she asked.

"This can't happen again."

"Why not?"

"It's not natural. What's happening isn't supposed to be possible."

What was he talking about? A chill went down her spine. He wasn't going to spoil this. She wouldn't let him. "This isn't where the dream goes scary again, is it? Because I've had enough of that."

He looked to where her fingers gripped his shoulders. "No, Sexy Red. Not scary."

He kissed her fingers softly and finally looked

into her eyes. "I have to leave you. I can't come back again—not like this."

Her jaw dropped. Why was he doing this? She'd dreamed about him for seven months. She wasn't letting him go now!

Brazenly, she dug her heels into his back. For all his words, she still felt his cock swell inside her. "You're mine," she said fervently.

His lips twisted into a forlorn smile. "Yeah, I think I am."

"I'm going to keep dreaming about you," she insisted.

"Dreaming," he repeated, shaking his head.

She felt him start to pull back.

"No. Stay with me tonight."

He disentangled her legs from his hips. "I can't."

She sat up. "Just a little while longer? In case you're right?"

She could see the battle inside him. Then his tension eased, and she knew she'd won.

"All right. Just for a little while."

She relaxed against him when his arms came back around her. Their bodies fit together so perfectly, it was heady.

"We'll see about tomorrow when it comes," she said, nipping at his neck.

He sighed. "Devon."

She let her hot breath hit his ear and felt a womanly sense of power when he shivered. "We'll just see."

Eight

Cael walked into Hooligan's Bar expecting to see Tony and Derek. What he didn't expect was Wes and Zane—and three more of his brothers crowded around the pool table.

"Shit." Apparently word had spread.

He wanted to turn around and head right back outside but he knew he had to face the music. His big announcement about Devon breaking into the dream realm had made everyone nervous. If the shoe were on the other foot, he'd be here tonight demanding answers.

Sighing heavily, he walked up to the bar.

He should have sat on the information until he'd known more. Devon wasn't a menace; she wasn't being controlled by anything. She just wanted to be with him. Now that his brothers knew what she could do, though, there was no hiding it. They deserved to be told the truth.

"Budweiser," he said to the bartender.

"Bottle or tap?"

"Make it both."

The man's eyebrows lifted, but he simply shrugged and turned to fill the order. By the time he set the mug on the bar, Derek was already at Cael's side.

"Here," Cael said, shoving the frothy beer to his right. "This is for you."

"For what?"

"To shut you up for as long as I can."

Derek accepted with a smirk but looked around the smoky room. "Do you have enough money on you to keep buying rounds for eight? Because it just might take more than one to shut us all up."

"Yeah, but you're the one with the quickest mind. If I can slow you down, it will take longer for the others to catch up." Cael took the bottle from the bartender and paid the bill. Turning, he leaned back against the bar. "Is there anyone in the family who doesn't know?"

Eight of them in one place at one time. Every Dream Wreaker in the county had shown up.

Derek chose a peanut from the bowl on the bar. "You did drop a bombshell last week."

Cael dug his heel a little deeper into the hardwood floor. "I know."

Hell, nobody had been more rocked by this whole thing than he had been. And last night with Devon had definitely blown his mind—but that was not a subject for family discussion.

He took a long pull on his beer and watched as Wes lined up the cue ball with a solid for the corner pocket. "I jumped the gun," he said quietly. "There's no reason to worry."

"Yeah?"

"Yeah. Drink your beer."

Derek didn't look so sure, but he glanced down at the mug in his hand. Tilting his head in acknowledgment, he kept his questions to himself.

Cael appreciated the reprieve.

Then he heard "Love Potion Number Nine" coming out of the old-fashioned jukebox. Ah, shit. "Zane!"

Laughter went up around the bar, and Wes looked up from the pool table where he was beating Tony. "So what's the deal with Sexy Red?" he called.

Half the bar turned in his direction, and Cael started a slow burn.

"Fuck," he muttered. Now that everyone had spotted him, they might as well get to it. He jerked his head toward the large round table in the corner.

Tony nodded and turned to put away his pool cue. The others followed his lead.

When eight men moved in one direction at one time, people noticed. Especially the women. Two barflies in a booth by the door started fluffing their hair and sticking out their cleavage when the first of them walked by. Bobby pivoted on his heel to say hello, but AJ caught him by the shoulder. "Just keep walking."

The busy barmaid wasn't as concerned with flirting. When she saw that the table they were heading for was still dirty, she scrambled to clean up the bottles the previous customers had left behind.

"Hey, gorgeous. Let me help," Zane said, cozying up to her to grab two empty mugs.

The pretty brunette rolled her eyes with impatience but bobbled her tray when she actually caught a good look at him. "Thanks," she said, a smile lighting her tired lips.

The table was quickly cleared, with Zane flirtily pulling the waitress's rag out from her belt and wiping off the table's crumbs.

"That's more work than I've seen you do in years," Tony teased as he pulled out a chair in the corner.

"Maybe if you had big blue eyes, I'd do favors for you, too." Zane winked at the waitress, who was handing out menus.

Cael shook his head. Their Oneiroi ancestors had been masters of assuming the human form. Over time they'd assimilated into human society, but there were still intrinsic differences. It was a Dream Wreaker's responsibility to blend in, but some of them did it better than others. Zane liked attention, preferably of the female variety.

"Bring us two pitchers on me," Cael ordered.

"And a pork tenderloin sandwich," Mack said. "I've got to get some food in me before I go to work."

Mack worked the night shift, which left him available to cover the day shift as a Dream Wreaker. Cael owed his brother for all the times he'd helped one of his charges who hadn't slept during the night.

Orders were placed for nachos and potato wedges and the waitress left. Tony leaned forward, bracing his elbows against the table, and his biceps bulged. "So what is the deal with Sexy Red?" he asked pointedly.

Cael took a quick look around the room to make sure there weren't any prying ears.

"She's a witch."

Seven pairs of blank eyes stared back at him.

"A witch?" Wes blurted.

Tony knocked him in the shoulder as nearly everyone else at the table hushed him. "Say it a little louder, why don't ya?"

Bobby shifted in his chair, and AJ looked around the room nervously.

"A witch," Tony repeated, loud enough for their table only. "Are you sure?"

Wind gusts? Color dancing on the walls? Energy surges? Oh yeah, Devon Bradshaw was a witch. "I'm sure."

His brothers looked at one another, trying to figure out what that meant for them, for the dream world, for the oh-so-important balance they worked so hard to keep . . .

"Good witch or bad?" Derek asked.

"White witch," Cael said with certainty. There was a little mischievousness inside her, maybe, but no evil. "But the funny thing is, I don't think she even knows."

"That she's good?" Derek said, his eyes narrowing.

"That she's a witch."

"How can that be?" Derek asked.

Cael shrugged. "I don't know, but she's got a lot of power, and it's growing."

Not only had she crossed into the dream realm before he'd led her into REM sleep, she'd kept her projection going after her first orgasm last night. And her second . . . and her third . . . That energy vortex in her kitchen was nothing to be trifled with.

"I don't know, Cael. A witch?" Tony shook his head. He started toying with the bottle of Tabasco sauce in the middle of the table. "They don't usually get involved with dream matters unless they're working with somebody who needs their special abilities. Somebody whose name usually rhymes with Lunatic."

Wes nodded. "I started asking around and there's been more dark activity lately. We're not the only ones who have sensed the energy shift."

"This spell is a little more complicated than I thought," Cael admitted. "It's binding me to her."

"You mean the *love* spell?" Zane asked.

Laughter sprung up again as Cael's brothers enjoyed his discomfort.

"Yes, the love spell," he growled.

"And you say there's bondage involved?" Zane continued.

The laughter got louder.

"Enough!" Cael warned.

Tony reached for his beer to hide his smile, but Wes and Zane still grinned.

Derek, meanwhile, was contemplative. "Are you sure she's not under the influence of anything? Lunatics? Somnambulists? Sandmen?"

Dream Wreakers walked a fine line in their efforts to maintain the status quo. Not only were they charged with keeping the balance for human emotions; they arbitrated the night. Too much control by the dark forces led to panic. Too much leeway for the Sandmen and people slept the day away.

"She's not being controlled by anything," Cael assured his brothers.

Except maybe passion, love, and romance . . .

He started fiddling with his coaster.

Derek cracked a peanut shell. Cael could practically see the gears in his head turning. "What does she think is happening?" he finally asked.

Cael scraped his thumbnail over the coaster's edge. "She just thinks she's dreaming."

"Awfully realistic dreams, I would think." Tony leaned back and crossed his arms over his chest. He still didn't look happy about things.

"Whatever she thinks, you need to stop it soon, Cael." Derek's brow furrowed. "You've been missing too many of your charges. I know, because I've been covering for you."

"Me, too," Wes said quietly.

"Yeah," Bobby agreed.

"I've been running my ass off," Tony said bluntly. "You need to step it up, big brother."

"I know," Cael said, his tone short. He didn't need them to tell him how to do his job. "I told her it won't be happening anymore."

"What exactly is *it*?" Zane asked.

Tony slowly turned his gaze on Cael, too. "Yes, what *is* happening between you two?"

The coaster crumpled in Cael's fist. "You don't want to go there."

Zane ignored the warning, curiosity plain on his face. "Holy shit, I was joking. Is it even possible? Can you *do* it in the dream realm?"

The joking at the table ceased, replaced by intense interest.

"Does it feel like the real deal? Man, two magical beings. Can you imagine?"

"Enough!" Cael smacked his hand down so hard on the heavy wooden table, it jumped. Having everyone pry into his sex life was one thing. Having them pry into Devon's was another entirely.

Zane fell back into his chair and urgent side discussions erupted.

Derek was undeterred. "I'm serious, Cael. You know what happens when people don't dream."

Cael knew all too well, and it kept him from enjoying Devon as fully as he wanted. There were evil people in the world, those truly touched by malevolence. It didn't matter how many dreams they dreamt, it wouldn't change them. For normal people, though, dreams helped them work out their deepest issues, confront their darkest fears. Dreams and nightmares kept the worst of human nature from the waking world. Without that internal therapy, people could go mad.

"Just a little longer," Cael said. "Then she won't need to visit me in her sleep."

"Cael," Derek pressed.

Tony suddenly saw the barmaid headed in their direction. "Food," he said.

All talk about dreams abruptly ended, and he smiled at the brunette. She smiled back as she set the potato wedges in front of him but threw a glance Zane's way. Apparently the idiot had caught her interest. Tony rolled his eyes.

Cael reached for his beer, wondering just how much mileage they were going to get out of this love spell thing. Too much, no doubt.

"So what *is* it like?" Derek asked quietly after the watress left. "Seriously."

Cael nearly dropped his bottle.

His usually reserved brother shrugged. "It's probably the best solution to an impossible problem, letting her think she's having erotic dreams."

Cael just stared at him.

"We're not eunuchs," Derek added softly, then raised his voice. "Hey, send those nachos down this way."

Food always seemed to break the strain at these family meetings, and tonight was no different. The subject was dropped as everyone started sharing the ketchup and the hot salsa.

Cael just wasn't in the mood for food. He'd known this discussion wasn't going to be pleasant, and he'd been right. When it came to Devon, things hit a little too close to home.

And he still hadn't figured out what he was going to do about *that*.

Seeing the mess he'd made of his coaster, he sighed. He laid it flat on the table and tried to smooth it out. That woman had him totally knotted up.

"Whoa," Tony suddenly said. "Hey, bartender," he yelled. "Turn that TV up."

Chairs scraped against the floor as everyone turned to look. A news report was on the screen. Cael listened, a warning signal pricking at the back of his neck, as the anchorman reported on a disturbance at the Happy Ranch fast-food restaurant. Apparently a customer had become so enraged with a teenage worker who couldn't make change, he'd jumped right over the counter and punched him. He'd proceeded to throw the entire cash drawer on the floor before running off with an armload of deep-fried apple pies.

Around the bar, patrons began to laugh. All Cael heard, though, was the sound of his pulse pounding in his ears. He tried to focus as the anchor went on to explain that the man was still on the loose. Authorities considered him mentally unstable and asked people to be on the alert.

"What's he going to do?" the bartender roared. "Stuff apple pies down our throats?"

By now, people were laughing as if they'd never heard anything so funny.

At Cael's table, though, nobody was smiling.

When they faced one another again, each one of them was dead serious.

"The full moon was last night," Bobby said.

"But he vaulted the counter at dinnertime, in full sunlight," Mack protested.

"Hold on, let's not jump the gun," Zane said. "The guy really could be crazy."

"Or maybe he just hasn't been dreaming." Tony turned. "Whose charge is he?"

Cael glanced up at the television, where Chet Watkins's face filled the screen. Chet Watkins, who loved his little twin girls. Chet, who was trying so desperately to lose those last fifteen pounds.

"Shit," he said underneath his breath. "He's mine."

Everyone looked at him, but nobody could say anything that would make him feel any worse than he already did. The balance had shifted—and his charges were suffering because of it. His fingers curled around the coaster, tearing it right in two. How could he have let this happen? These people were under his care!

Icy determination settled in his chest. "I need one of you to take over as Devon's Dream Wreaker."

"Are you sure?" Tony asked.

As much as he didn't want to, Cael nodded. "Just do it."

It was past time he took care of his own. All of them.

The world was going crazy.

It was the only reason Jason Rappaport could come up with as he looked at a woman trying to fly a kite in the middle of the street. Absolutely crazy. He shook his head as a policeman struggled to get her out of traffic.

The poor guy looked as tired as he felt.

Sighing, he rolled his aching shoulders. Everyone he knew was tired. Every night, they were getting called to more and more accidents and fight scenes. And the reasons behind the incidents were getting stranger and stranger. Falling over footstools, fighting over peanut butter sandwiches, throwing a fit over a little noise . . .

A smile pulled at his lips as he remembered Tasha accosting him in little more than her birthday suit. Maybe not all those strange encounters were so bad.

"No, not bad at all," he told himself as he walked down Delano Street. Looking up, he saw a sign declaring St. James Designs in big, curly letters. In all the chaos, his raven-haired neighbor had been an intriguing find. Especially after the elevator . . .

Oh yeah, the elevator.

Stepping up to the front door, he eyed the place. As much as he'd enjoyed that spicy encounter, he was worried about the little minx. She'd fallen asleep on her feet. He needed to make sure she was all right.

"Here goes nothing," he said as he shifted the bag he was carrying. Reaching out, he knocked on the door.

Who knew what kind of greeting he'd get today?

A guy could only hope . . .

He waited, but nobody came to the door.

Confused, he looked at the hours posted in the front window. It would be a while before the shop opened, but Mrs. Howell had said that she'd seen Tasha leave earlier this morning. She should be here. Looking inside, he saw lights.

He knocked again, this time more loudly.

When nobody answered, he became uneasy. Going

with his gut, he reached for the door handle. It was unlocked.

The door let out a squeak as he pushed it open. With all the unrest in the city, she shouldn't leave her doors unlocked. It just wasn't safe.

"Tasha?" he called as he stepped inside.

The studio was a big open space with a counter, a desk, and a huge conference table up front. The rest of the area was filled with shelving, art supplies, and tools. Paintings were tucked here and there, with protective cloths covering some. Others looked to be half finished.

"Whirlwind?" he called again.

He didn't like the silence.

He started heading toward the back. "Ta—"

A hollow crash suddenly split the air. Almost instantly he started running. "Tasha!" he called as he rounded a corner into the back room.

Her hair whipped around her shoulders as she turned toward him. Her eyes went wide, but then recognition hit. "You!"

Jason's brain stalled. Absolutely hit the brakes and skidded to a stop.

She was naked.

Stark, butt naked.

"What are you doing here?" she asked suspiciously.

With effort, he shut his mouth before he started to drool. "Looking for you."

And man, had he found her.

Unable to stop himself, he let his gaze slide over her. Her dark hair contrasted sharply with her perfect, translucent skin, the tresses hanging down around her shoulders and over her chest.

She was small, but her body was tight. Her lines were sleek, but curvy in all the right places. He stared at her breasts and saw her nipples playing peek-a-boo through the curtain of her hair. Just looking at the tiny nubs made his mouth water.

As did the smooth, well-groomed vee of hair at the apex of her legs.

He stared at her unabashedly, and his eyes nearly bugged out of his head when she bent over to right a paint can.

"Fuck," he whispered. Was she trying to kill him?

She glanced over her shoulder, her eyes narrowing dangerously. "You found me. What do you want with me?"

Oh, hell. Unfair question.

"I had to work late," he said, the words stumbling over his tongue. He forced his gaze to her face so he could think halfway clearly. "When I got home, I noticed you weren't there. Mrs. Howell told you'd come down here early, so I thought maybe we could share some breakfast."

"That busybody," Tasha said. She dipped a paintbrush in the can at her feet and spun around. Winding up like an ace relief pitcher, she flung her arm at the canvas in front of her. Blue paint flew from her brush. It hit hard, and blue droplets splattered everywhere.

Jason went still. The act had been almost violent.

He took a step back, remembering the paintings he'd seen up front. They'd been incredibly beautiful, almost painstakingly detailed. Uneasiness caught him. "Is this, uh . . . your normal technique?"

"No!"

When she looked over her shoulder, though, her face was clear and innocent.

"Do you like it?" she asked.

She'd gone from defensive to needy in a split second. Something was off here. Very off.

He looked again at her "work." The canvas was awash in blues, yellows, and reds. Lots and lots of reds. It reminded him too much of the bad night he'd had. Accidents galore and a suicide attempt. "It's very . . . colorful."

"I hate it," she said matter-of-factly. She walked to the canvas, her bottom swaying sexily with each step. "I think I'm going to call it *Insomnia*."

His focus sharpened. When she turned around, this time all he saw was her face. "Are you still not sleeping?"

She shrugged. "Sometimes. I just don't get any rest."

Turning back toward the canvas, she wiped the brush across the tableau with a vicious stroke.

Jason set the food down on the shelf beside him.

Watching his steps on the paint-streaked drop cloth, he headed toward her. "Why didn't you come tell me about this?"

He caught her by the arm when she tried to scamper away.

She looked at his fingers circling her bicep, and an entirely different emotion played across her pretty little face.

"Mmmm," she purred. "So strong and commanding." She looked up at him. "Are you a dom, Mr. Noisy?"

He slid a hand through her hair to hold her still. The circles under her eyes were almost purple, and lines of fatigue marred her forehead and radiated from her mouth.

Her full, enticing mouth.

He rubbed his thumb across her lips gently. "Tasha, this is getting serious. We need to get you to a doctor."

Her dark eyes flared. "Pill pusher!"

She whirled away and raced toward a can of red paint. He barely ducked in time as paint flew over his head. Still, the spray spattered his hair and shoulders. "Hey!" he yelled.

The noise surprised her. She blinked and looked from him to the canvas. The shock on her face couldn't be faked. "I'm . . . I'm sorry." She backed away from him, embarrassment and dismay on her face. "I don't know what I'm doing!"

The paintbrush fell wetly to the floor. Turning, she walked shakily to the opposite corner, where a clay sculpture stood.

Jason threw a glance at the thing but then couldn't look away. It gave him the creeps. Twisty and contorted, it looked like something out of a horror movie. He actually moved toward Tasha to stop her when she reached out to stroke it.

"I'm being mean to you . . . to Devon . . ." She glanced his way. "I can't stop it. It just comes out."

The hair at the back of his neck rose. He knew that lack of sleep could do strange things to a person. It could affect rational thoughts and cause emotions to swing, but what he was seeing was extreme.

"It's okay," he said, moving closer. "I'm thick skinned."

"You shouldn't have to be." Her fingers trailed over the head of the . . . thing. Its mouth was open as if in a howl.

"My head hurts," she whispered, "and so does my body. All I want to do is sleep. Why can't I sleep?"

The protective feeling that came over him was downright dangerous. "Let me take you to see somebody. I'll get you right past the waiting room."

All of her muscles clenched.

"No."

"Why not?"

Her fingers wrapped around the ghostly object's neck. "No pills. I can't. *I won't.*"

"But why? They'll help you."

"They'll hook me!"

Her yell reverberated in the air. She took a step back in surprise. Looking away in shame, she raked an unsteady hand through her hair. It swept the long strands back, exposing her totally.

Jason's cock roared with wanting, but she was revealing more to him than just her body.

He took another step forward. "What was it?" he asked quietly.

Unwillingly, she glanced down. When she did, she suddenly realized she was naked. "Oh, damn."

She seemed more put out than embarrassed. That was fine with him. She could go naked around him all she wanted but, right now, he was looking over her with the eye of an EMT—and he was jaded enough to expect the worst. His gaze skimmed her body, looking for track marks or collapsed veins . . .

Her knee. His stomach clenched. The scars were faded, so the surgery must have been a while ago. From a distance, only somebody like him would even notice them.

"Pain pills?" he said, knowing the pattern all too well.

He found a painter's smock on a chair and took it over to her.

She nodded as he put it over her shoulders. "The doctor said those would help, too, and he just kept writing that damn prescription."

"What happened?" Jason asked, rubbing her shoulders gently.

"I was a dancer when I was younger, but my knee wasn't up to it."

"You seem to have rehabbed okay." She didn't limp, and she had full range of motion. He should know. He'd been watching her closely enough.

"Yes, though the physical therapy was a bitch." She threw a sidelong look at the sculpture. "The withdrawal was worse."

And when people thought of medications that might be habit-forming, sleeping pills were right up there with pain pills.

Jason looked again at the sculpture and finally got it. She was afraid of losing control. The thing seemed to ripple before his eyes, and he wanted to throw it out the window.

"Tasha," he said, running a hand through his hair.

He really didn't think she realized the seriousness of the situation. Something could be wrong with her thalamus. Her immune system might be weakened. If she was having microsleep sessions, she could fall asleep at the driver's wheel—or the pottery wheel tucked in the corner of the room.

Yeah, best not to think about that.

"You just need to tell your physician all this," he said as persuasively as he could. "He'll be more careful when he prescribes something for the insomnia. Whirlwind, you've got to do *something*."

She flung her hands up into the air. "Do you think I haven't tried?"

He could see the stubbornness in the set of her jaw. As much as he was tempted to pick her up, toss her over his shoulder, and carry her right down to the hospital, it wouldn't work. Letting out a steadying breath, he made himself back off.

"I didn't come here to fight with you." He shrugged and gestured toward the brown paper bag. "Like I said, I brought you breakfast."

Her head cocked. "As in food?"

He blinked. These mood swings were something else. "Bagels and coffee. Decaf," he said quickly.

He opened the bag and pulled out two coffees, the bagels, and cream cheese, and set them on the shelf.

He almost jumped out of his skin when Tasha brushed up against him to see what he was doing. He could feel her breasts cushioned against his rib cage and her knee sliding up his thigh.

"Plain or blueberry?" he asked tightly.

"What else do you have in there?" she asked curiously.

He whipped the bag away. "Nothing."

"Oh, come on," she said, reaching around him.

He determinedly rolled the top shut. "That's it."

Holding him about the waist, she squeezed between him and the shelf. "I don't think so."

He held the bag higher, and a devilish look entered her brown eyes. She was already rubbing against him suggestively. Watching him boldly, she reached down for the fly of his jeans and cupped him.

The feel of her tiny hand grinding against his half-solid erection made Jason drop the sack. It hit the floor with a thud, and a bottle tumbled out.

A bottle of chocolate syrup.

He looked at it. Then at her. Then at the bottle again.

"It was a joke," he said hurriedly. "In case you were feeling better."

She jerked down the zipper of his jeans.

"So which is it?" She smiled silkily. "A joke? Or in case I was feeling better?"

She thrust her hand inside and began to stroke him. He gritted his teeth so hard, stars nearly exploded in front of his eyes.

But she's not feeling well, a voice called from the back of his mind. She's not thinking clearly. He needed to stop her.

So why couldn't he move?

She let out a giggle as she hooked her leg around his. When her heel dug into the back of his knee, his leg buckled.

"Tasha!"

She pushed against his chest determinedly, and he couldn't stop it. He was going down.

And she still had his dick in a death grip.

Grabbing her by the ass, he took her down with

him. He landed on his butt on the paint-speckled drop cloth, and she came down in his lap.

Straddling him, she undulated sexily. "I think I'm feeling better."

"Tasha, wait," he said when she started to push him onto his back.

Reaching out, he grabbed her by the shoulders.

He was left holding only her smock when she shimmied right out of it.

One look at her, and he was stopped cold. God, she was the most gorgeous thing he'd ever seen. Looks, spirit, and sass all rolled up into one. And that body of hers . . . He broke out in a cold sweat.

She leaned forward to kiss him, and he caught her by the waist. He meant to push her off of him, but the moment he touched her soft skin, he forgot his intentions.

The girl knew how to kiss.

Their mouths went at each other's, suckling, rubbing, and nipping. They outright sucked face until he felt the head of his cock push against her warm pussy. She'd worked him out of his briefs and was squirming on top of him.

"Tasha," he groaned.

The EMT inside of him knew she wasn't thinking straight. She'd hate him eventually if he took advantage of her.

He wasn't given much say in the matter, though,

when she yanked his T-shirt out of his jeans and squirted chocolate syrup on his stomach.

"Mmm," she said dreamily, diving down for a taste.

His hand fisted in her hair. Oh, Christ. He wasn't a saint.

She pushed his T-shirt higher, trying to get it out of her way, and he jerked it over his head. Chocolate hit his left nipple. When her hot tongue rasped over it, he was a goner.

Rolling with her in his arms, he squirted chocolate sauce all over her front and began to feast.

It was a free-for-all from there on out.

His jeans went flying. Chocolate squirted. Tongues licked. Mouths sucked. Jason didn't know which was sweeter, the syrup or her body.

And she was everywhere. She moved like a blur, and everything she did was sexual. She squirmed. She sighed. She raked her fingernails down his thighs. Together, they rolled naked on the floor, picking up splotches of paint as they went.

"Give me that," she said yanking the bottle out of his hand. Suddenly, Jason couldn't breathe. She was looking at his cock with the most dangerous intention sparkling in her eyes.

Even knowing what she was going to do, he bucked when she squirted chocolate directly on his privates. The cold made his balls draw up tight. Nothing prepared him, though, for the sight of her leaning down over him and licking her lips in anticipation.

She started with the underside of his cock, and the sensation made his hips roll. She wasn't deterred. Seeking out every last drop, she licked and licked and licked. One of his hands tangled in her hair. The other clung to the drop cloth so tightly, he heard it rip.

She finally settled over the head of his erection. Looking down, he saw her head bobbing up and down over him. She was taking more of his throbbing cock into her throat with every suckle.

"Enough," he rasped. Catching her under the armpits, he pulled her off of him.

She let out a peal of laughter as they rolled on the floor again. "I told you chocolate was better than vanill-ahh!"

He'd thrust his fat, hungry cock into her right to the hilt. And, oh God, was she creamy.

"You were right," he grunted, thrusting harder and harder.

"Mmmm," she crooned. She wrapped her arms and legs around him and began to lift her hips in time with his rhythm. "I know."

The drop cloth was slippery against the floor. With every thrust, they slid back and forth. Mostly forth. When her head bumped against the wall, Jason braced a hand on it for leverage.

"Yes!" she gasped as he banged into her harder and harder.

He buried his face in the crook of her neck and felt her fingernails rake down his back. Everywhere their bodies touched, they were hot and sticky. Sticky with sweat, with chocolate, with paint.

It was a wham-bam of a fuck, but Jason couldn't help it.

She'd jumped *him.*

He thrust hard one more time, and her body jack-knifed underneath him.

He ejaculated so hard, he felt a bite at the base of his spine. And it went on and on. When it finally let him go, every muscle in his body fell limp.

"Christ," he said, fighting for air.

Her breaths puffed against his neck. Rolling with her in his arms, he took his weight off of her. She felt pliant against him, almost heavy.

As heavy as a featherweight could feel.

He brushed back her hair. "Tasha?" he said softly.

She didn't respond.

Concerned, he lifted his head off the floor. Her deep, steady breaths and completely relaxed position told him she hadn't collapsed or passed out.

She was asleep.

Dead-to-the-world asleep.

"I'll be damned," he whispered. He brushed his fingers over her soft cheek.

Her eyelashes fanned out over the dark circles under her eyes, and her relaxed lips softened the lines around her mouth. Something in his chest tightened, and he brushed a kiss across her forehead.

His cock was still buried inside her, but he wasn't moving for the life of him.

Looking around, he saw his T-shirt nearby. Taking care not to rouse her, he reached for it. Wadding it up, he stuck it under his head as a pillow. He didn't care if the front door was unlocked. He was staying put until they'd both gotten a good ten hours of sleep.

After all, he'd come here wanting to help.

If this was the only way she'd let him, so be it. He was definitely up to the task.

Nine

Devon could hear her phone ringing as she climbed the back steps of her house. She'd had to work late again, and she'd forgotten to leave the porch light on. It made it difficult to see as she stuck the key into the lock. Hurriedly, she let herself in and made a mad dash to the cordless in the kitchen. "Hello?" she answered breathlessly.

"Oh, thank God. I finally found you."

"Tasha? What's wrong?"

"I've been trying to reach you on your cell phone for hours!"

"It's not working." Devon slid her purse off one shoulder and her camera equipment off the other. She didn't like the sound of her friend's voice. "Are you okay?"

"I've been worried about you. I heard about the bank holdup next to the *Sentinel*."

"Everybody's fine," Devon reassured her. "I wasn't even there."

She'd been out shooting the nine-car pileup on the freeway. It had been bad—but Tasha didn't need to know that, not with her nerves already strung tight.

Feeling jittery herself, Devon turned to the refrigerator, pulled out a bottle of wine, and opened the cupboard for a glass. "How have *you* been?" she asked.

Their conversation the other day still bothered her. That, and that eerie maquette. If she hadn't been working overtime, she would have called Tasha earlier to check on her.

"I'm better, I think."

Devon stopped with the wineglass halfway to her lips. "Did you get some sleep?"

"A little, with Jason. I think I might have even dreamed."

"Tasha, that's great!" So the paramedic was still in the picture. It was good to know she wasn't losing her touch entirely. She'd asked around, and Rappaport was known to be one of the best at what he did. Knowing he was watching over her friend made her feel better.

Yet Tasha let out a sigh. "We only managed to get about two hours before a customer woke us up. Let me tell you, *that* was entertaining. Last night, though, wasn't so good. I tossed and turned until dawn."

"Me, too," Devon confessed.

"You didn't sleep?"

Damn. She shouldn't have said anything. "Not very well."

"What did he do?"

Devon rubbed her temple. Apparently two hours of sleep wasn't enough to wipe out paranoia. "My dream man didn't show."

Instead, a different man had stood by her bedside.

She hadn't liked that at all.

"But that's fantastic!" Tasha said, her mood brightening instantly. "Those dreams needed to stop a long time ago. You were getting way too tied up in them."

Devon twirled her wineglass by the stem. Maybe she had been, but what was wrong with that? All she saw during the day were accidents, crimes, and pain.

"Do you think our problems are over?" Tasha asked excitedly. "The moon is finally full."

Devon looked out the window over her kitchen sink. Nightfall was deepening. Every time evening rolled around, she could feel her impatience growing, the darkness pulling at her.

Calling her . . .

Suddenly, she felt energy in her fingertips.

She looked at the wineglass stem and, for a split second, could have sworn it was glowing. She quickly set it down.

" 'It' hasn't told me anything," she said. "Good or bad."

"No? But I thought—"

"Let's schedule a spa day," Devon said impulsively. "We both need to relax. We could get a massage or herbal wrap and sleep the rest of the afternoon."

"Oh, that sounds like heaven."

"I'll see if I can get something scheduled for this weekend."

"Okay."

"Sleep tight tonight," Devon said, truly meaning it.

"I'll try."

"Call me if you need anything."

"I will, Mother Hen. Bye."

"Bye." Devon hung up and stared intently at her wineglass. It looked innocent enough, but she knew what she'd seen.

And she knew what she felt.

She opened and closed her hand, but her fingers still buzzed. Curious, she dug her cell phone out of her purse and pressed the power button. The screen stayed blank. When she'd picked it up earlier this afternoon, her fingertips had prickled with a surge and her phone had gone out.

She looked outside again at the moon. It was big and bright as a beacon. "Are you causing all of this?"

Feeling unsettled, she turned away from the window. It put the kitchen table into full view.

She sagged back against the counter. Two nights

later, she was still stunned by her fevered dream. Talk about energy flashes! So much power had snapped around her and her dream man, she was surprised her house hadn't come down around them. She'd certainly woken up believing it had really happened, *feeling* as if it had really happened.

She watched as she curled her fingers in toward her palm. She still felt energized, as if something inside her had been awakened.

She glanced at the stove. Maybe it wasn't a coincidence that her dream had occurred here in the kitchen. Something *had* happened with that spell.

"Something strong," she whispered.

The sensation in this room was unmistakable. She felt it every time she walked in. Impulsively, she reached out her hand. She couldn't have been more surprised when a dart of blue passed through her peripheral vision.

"*What?*" Her head snapped to the side.

No, it couldn't have been. Still, she felt a tingle—the same tingle she'd felt at the greenhouse.

It wasn't good; it wasn't bad. It was just there.

Watching closely, she lifted her hand again. She nearly fell on the floor when shimmers of purple and green scampered across the ceiling.

"Oh, my God!"

Her heart began to race, and she flung out her hand like a magician. She heard a sizzle, then a flare of hot pink jumped on the far wall.

Devon jumped nearly as high when she heard the slam of the doggie door.

"Damn it, Cedric! One day you're going to give me a heart attack."

The beagle let out a whimper.

"It's all right," she said as she squatted down to greet him. "You just surprised me."

He backed away from her, and his ears flopped as he nervously surveyed the room.

They said that animals were more sensitive than people.

Warily, Devon looked again at the far wall. The tingle in her belly became a steady hum. She rubbed it, and her fingers sizzled. Apprehension suddenly filled her.

She shook off the sensation. She was only scaring herself. With things in the world spiraling out of control, it was too easy to let her thoughts go to dark places. There had to be a logical explanation. Maybe there was something wrong with the electrical system. She'd been having problems with the air conditioner.

"Come here, buddy," she said, patting her hands together.

He flinched.

"Cedric. It's me."

He whined and began sniffing the air.

Devon walked over to the cupboard and found a treat. When she turned the light on, the dog finally seemed to relax. Still, his approach was cautious before he took the snack out of her hands and settled onto the floor.

Devon scratched the top of his head. "You're feeling the strange vibrations in the air, too, aren't you, buddy?"

Everywhere she'd gone today, she'd felt weird and out of sync.

More and more, the outside world felt foreign to her. The only place she really felt safe these days was tucked in her own bed, asleep in her own dreams.

Absently, she brushed her fingers across the table. She felt safe with *him*.

"Let yourself out when you're done," she told the dog as she gave him a final pat. It was early, but she didn't care. She'd worked late, she was tired, and tomorrow was a big day. She needed to be at her best.

She was going to bed.

He wasn't there.

Devon knew it the moment she opened her eyes. The moonlight was murkier than it had been earlier. She looked into the dark corners, but still couldn't see him. Much more, she couldn't feel him.

"Dreamer?" she whispered.

The only thing she heard was the click of the air conditioner as it cycled on. As she watched, the curtains over the far vent began to sway like billowing ghosts.

She looked away. It reminded her too much of Tasha's sculpture.

Instead, she focused on the ceiling, feeling disappointed. As happy as her friend had been, she didn't want the recurring dream to stop. With all the strange things happening in her waking life, her dreams were the only retreat she had.

She closed her eyes again. She just wanted to escape. Was that too much to ask?

"Come be with me," she whispered. When she glanced about the room again, though, it hadn't changed. She was just as alone as she'd ever been.

But that was nothing new, was it? He'd never really been here in the first place.

Loneliness welled up inside Devon's chest, and she rolled onto her side.

Bunching up her pillow, she tried to get more comfortable. So what if he was just a dream? He was *her* dream. Maybe if she relaxed and focused really hard, she could bring him back.

Calming herself, she thought of her nighttime lover. It wasn't difficult. She remembered his eyes . . . his dark hair . . . his wicked mouth . . .

Her baby doll nightie slid against her thigh as she drew up her knee. She'd read about directed dreams in her research. People often used them to solve problems—and she definitely had a problem.

His kisses . . . his hands . . .

The room was getting warmer, and she kicked off the sheet. She just needed to fall asleep thinking about him and let her subconscious mind take over.

She felt herself sink deeper into the mattress as she pictured his wide shoulders, his rock hard abs, and—

She squirmed on the bed.

—*his rock hard cock.*

Rolling onto her back, she pressed the back of her hand against her forehead. She wanted to see him. She wanted to talk to him.

"Lead me to my heart's desire."

Deeper and deeper she drifted until she felt herself almost floating. The sensation was pleasant, and she gave herself over to it. Her body felt light, airy. A warm breeze danced over her skin, and something prickly touched the bottoms of her feet.

Devon opened her eyes and gasped. She was no longer in her bedroom; she was standing on damp, freshly cut grass. "Solstice City Park?"

Confused, she looked around. The center fountain was gurgling away happily. She heard crickets chirping and the colors were muted under the artificial light of streetlamps. She looked at the flowers. The blooms were closed upon themselves, awaiting the first hint of sunlight.

She looked around in wonder. Everything seemed crisp. Precise. There wasn't a detail out of place.

But why was she here?

She began to walk along the curving sidewalk that meandered through the gardens. She'd barely gotten around the first wide arc when she saw him.

It worked—she'd found him!

The streetlight lit her dream man's powerful form as he stood over a park bench. The fluorescent light made his dark hair glint. His feet were bare and he wore pajama bottoms, but from the waist up he was naked. Her fingers began to itch just looking at his rippling chest.

Suddenly, he felt her presence. He looked up, and her breath caught.

His dark, slashing stare rooted her where she stood. He looked so fierce and aggressive, it frightened her. Defensively, her hands came up. She stepped back when he made a motion toward her. In that same moment, though, he realized who she was.

"Red? But how . . ." He let out a curse and ran a hand through his rumpled hair. Emotions flitted across his face, then his jaw hardened. "Damn it. I told you we couldn't do this anymore."

Why was he angry? "But—"

"But nothing. The other night was it. I told you that."

She blinked. *Well, hello to you, too.* "I do have some say in this. It's *my* dream."

He stalked toward her. "No, you don't. I can't spend time with you anymore. I have responsibilities, Red. You can't be here."

"But I am here," she snapped. "I had a bad day, and I wanted a nice dream to chase it away. So sue me."

He looked at her sharply, concern replacing his anger. "Did something happen? What's wrong?"

"Everything," she said, dropping her hands to her sides.

He stepped closer. "You look pale."

"That's because I'm tired and scared."

"Of me? Ah Red, I didn't mean to—"

"Not of you." The dream was so real, she felt the chill in the air. Wrapping her arms around herself, she tried to chase it away. "It's the waking world."

He stiffened. "Did somebody hurt you? Frighten you?"

Memories of the car wreck came back to her. Mangled metal, crying children, crunching glass . . . Nobody had been seriously hurt, but seeing the aftermath of such violence had gotten to her.

"I had a difficult shoot today." She shook her head. "Something's not right. I can see it happening through the lens of my camera. People are turning wild, mean. It's getting so that the only place I feel safe is with you."

He let out a long breath. "So you're sensing it, too—the disharmony, the discord."

"That's *exactly* what it is."

Nothing was working together as it should. It was like a song where the notes suddenly weren't matching the chords. The timing was off, and the melody clashed. People needed to get in tune with one another again.

But how?

Suddenly, Devon flinched. She hadn't realized they

weren't alone. There was a man sleeping on the bench her dream man had been standing over. She peered closer. "Oh, my God. Is that the mayor?"

Her dream man caught her hand. "Let's take a walk."

"It is!" She looked over her shoulder as he began to lead her away. With no shoes on his feet and a newspaper for a pillow, their dignified mayor looked like a homeless person. "Damn, where is my camera when I need it?"

"This is a dream."

"Well, yes, but I could still dream myself a money shot."

He shook his head, and she thought she saw a smile pull at his lips. It disappeared quickly, though, and he guided her farther down the path.

"How did you find me, Sexy Red?"

She looked down at their joined hands. They fit together perfectly, just like the rest of their bodies did. She blushed and glanced away.

"I just wished for it," she said. The hem of her short baby doll brushed against the side of his thigh with every step. "I directed my dream."

"You directed yourself, all right," he said, rubbing his thumb against the back of her hand. "You're getting too powerful for your own good. Sensing me . . . sensing the dissonance . . ."

"I've always been able to sense you."

Their gazes caught, and his grip on her hand tightened.

"Devon," he said, his voice low. "Did your mother or father ever do things like the love spell you told me about?"

He was looking at her so intently, heat unfurled in her belly. "Are you asking me if they met after performing a love spell?"

"No," he said evasively. "Did either of them like to do things to entertain you as a kid? Like magic shows or . . ."

He stopped to pick a shiny penny up from off the ground. "Or make a penny appear from behind your ear?"

"I don't remember anything like that," she said, taking the penny when he handed it to her. She rubbed her thumb over Lincoln's profile. Heads up. That meant good luck. She could use a bit of good luck right now.

She folded the penny into her hand. "My grandmother told me fairy tales about mystical beings and enchanted lands, though." She cocked her head consideringly. "She was the only one who encouraged me to trust in my inner sense."

"Your inner sense?" He came to a stop.

She turned, and the soft nighttime breeze caught her short hemline. It floated upward, and his dark gaze naturally snapped down. He went dead still when he realized she wasn't wearing any panties.

Devon swallowed hard and fought not to cover herself. "The last ones were ruined when I woke up," she said at barely a whisper.

His gaze locked with hers again, and it was blistering hot. When he stepped closer and cupped her cheek, her pulse took off.

"Tell me about this inner sense."

His voice rumbled across her skin. Goose bumps popped up everywhere the breeze could touch, but Devon's tension was magnified by something else entirely. She'd never told anyone other than her family and Tasha about "it." Could she trust him?

She looked into his stern, handsome face. He was a figment of her imagination. She had to keep reminding herself of that, but it was true.

"Tell me," he said softly.

Her hand clutched the penny until its edges bit into her skin. "I know things sometimes."

"Like other people's thoughts? Are you clairvoyant?"

Hesitantly, she took his hand and pressed it flat against her belly. "I feel it right here when something bad is going to happen. I get an ache that almost doubles me over."

A zap of electricity coursed down between her legs, and she squeezed her thighs together reflexively. His fingers pressed harder, as if wanting to take that pain away.

The action made her throat constrict with emotion.

"I feel good things, too," she said hoarsely. "Though lately, there haven't been many of them."

"But you're feeling the energy shift."

She nodded.

"Damn," he said softly. His fingers curved around her waist, and his thumb stroked over her belly button. "How bad is it?"

"Pretty bad."

"Do you see what's causing it?"

She looked at him, confusion knotting her brow. "I don't actually see anything. I just . . ."

"You feel," he said, somehow understanding. He let out a heavy breath and pulled her into his arms.

Impulsively, she wrapped her arms around his neck. He wasn't looking at her as if she was crazy; he was acting as if he empathized with how she felt. Lifting herself up onto her tiptoes, she kissed him. He let out a low groan before opening his mouth and kissing her back.

He tried to keep it slow. She let him, but she wouldn't allow him to bank the heat. She needed the heat. She needed him.

"You can't come for me like this," he said, even as his hands slid up the back of her thighs to cup her bare bottom. "You need to stop 'dreaming' about me."

Devon shivered when his fingers dipped into the crease between her buttocks. "You'd prefer that I dream about the man who came to me last night?"

His head snapped up. "You saw To——, someone else?"

Ah, she liked his jealousy. She brushed her fingers over his shoulders and let her tongue slide across the pulse at the side of his neck. "Somebody else was at my bedside. I knew as soon as I felt him that it wasn't you."

"Damn," he muttered under his breath.

Devon pulled back to look at him. "He was naked," she said, upping the stakes.

Her dream man's dark eyes flared, and his grip on her tightened. *"He came to you naked?"*

Devon nearly moaned. The way he was holding her bottom was making her wet.

"He was hot," she said, trying to find her breath. "If I'd stared long enough, I might have started drooling on my pillow."

His fingers dug into her cheeks, pulling her hips forward.

"But I didn't," she gasped. Her belly was rubbing a very big, very hard erection. She stroked her hands across her dream man's chest and felt his heart thudding underneath her palm. They were done, huh?

She kissed his chest and pressed her hips against him. "He was surprised when he realized I could see him. It was a great dream, really. He went to cover his . . . uh, package . . . and I went to push him away. I didn't even touch him, but he went flying. He vaporized—kind of like you do—as he went through the door."

The look on her dream man's face was indescribable. Shaking his head, he sat down hard on a park bench and pulled her on top of him. "I guess *that's* not going to work."

She straddled his lap and met his gaze steadily. "I only want you in my bedroom."

"From now on, I'll be the one who comes to you."

"You promise?"

"I promise." He rubbed her bare ass possessively. "That was a powerful love spell you cast, Sexy Red. I can't seem to stay away from you."

She reached for the tie of his pajama bottoms. "I can't stay away from you, either. I need to be with you."

Her fingers wrapped around his cock, and his head fell back.

"We'll be together." He let out a groan as she began to pump him. "You'll see me again before you know it."

Ten

"What the *hell* were you thinking, Tony?" Cael asked as he took the Mars Street exit into downtown. "You went to Devon naked?"

"Well yeah, but . . . you don't understand."

"*Naked?*"

"It wasn't like that."

"What *was* it like? I ask you to do one thing, and you flash my girl?"

"I didn't flash anything. I sleep in the buff!"

"You couldn't have put on some boxers? Shit!" Cael jammed on the brakes when a red sports car cut in front of him. The driver had the balls to flip him off. He looked quickly into his mirror and saw the cars behind him narrowly miss a chain-reaction pileup. Letting out a hiss of air, he switched into the next lane. "You know she can travel into the dream realm anytime she wants."

"No, I didn't know that. I thought maybe it only worked with you, Mr. Love Spell."

Cael gritted his teeth. He was never going to hear the end of that. "Well, now you know."

Tony let out a sigh. "If it makes you feel any better, she scared me as much as I scared her. I freaked out when she projected and split apart like that. It was like watching a spirit rise from a corpse when she sat up and gave me the evil eye."

"You *were* naked."

"Zheesh, let it go already. She obviously didn't like what she saw."

Which was the only thing that was saving Tony from a world of hurt. But from the tone of his brother's voice, Cael could tell his pride had been wounded. "Get out of the gym, Tony. She said you were hot."

"She did?" Tony said, perking up.

"Don't let it go to your head—and don't do it again."

His brother let out a derisive snort. "If you want someone to act as her Dream Wreaker, you're going to have to find a bigger fool. I'm not getting within fifty feet of your fiery witch; she nearly put my ass right through the wall."

Cael stopped at a red light. "What do you mean?"

"Sexy Red flung her hand at me when I surprised her. All I saw was orange sparks as something knocked me silly. I might have gotten a concussion if I hadn't dispersed as I was flying toward the door."

Cael looked down at his hands-free cell phone unit. "Are you serious?"

Horns sounded behind him as the light turned green.

"You think I would lie about something like that?"

Cael stepped on the gas when the driver behind him started shouting obscenities. He raked his hand through his hair. He'd known Devon's power was growing; she'd projected halfway across town to find him last night. He hadn't realized, though, that she was beginning to develop other abilities. "She still thinks she's dreaming."

"You've got to do something about her," Tony said, his voice turning serious. "With everything that's going on, she shouldn't be in the dream realm at all. It's not safe, Cael."

"I know. She knows it, too. She can feel the upheaval." Hell, everyone was feeling the upheaval. He looked at the rush-hour traffic around him. It was getting downright lethal.

"Something's got to give, and soon," Tony said quietly. "I'm having a hard time keeping up with my charges."

Cael felt a gnawing in his gut. All his brothers were

working overtime to pick up the charges he was missing. In the process, they were missing some of their own. "I'm hoping to get some things solved today."

"Oh, hey, that's right. Today's the big day."

More like the BIG day.

Cael finally arrived at his destination and entered the parking lot. A new day, a new job, a new start. Adrenaline started coursing through his system.

"Good luck, man. I hope everything goes all right."

"Me, too," Cael said as he parked. He turned off the engine and sat for a moment as he waited for his pulse to slow down. Today was important on so many levels. "It *has* to go all right."

He didn't know what he'd do if it didn't.

"I'm late, I know," Devon said as she rushed to her desk. Her purse whapped against her back as she skidded to a stop. Opening the bottom drawer, she dropped it inside.

"Where have you been?" George asked, looking at his watch. "It's almost time for the staff meeting."

"I overslept." Taking more care, she set down her camera equipment.

"Overslept?"

The disbelief in the older man's voice made Devon look over her shoulder. She found everyone in the room looking at her. "It happens."

"No, it doesn't. Not these days."

"I don't need a lecture, George," Devon said, stress entering her voice. She'd been working overtime, just like everyone else. She was tired. She hadn't even heard her alarm clock this morning. "I need my notebook."

"You're actually sleeping?" Jeannie asked, coming closer. She saw the way Devon was scanning her desk and pulled the notebook out from under a stack of proofs. "Here it is."

"Oh, thanks." Devon tucked it under her arm but still felt like she was missing something. She hated being late; it put her whole day out of whack. "Yeah, I'm sleeping. That's all I seem to be doing these days."

"Wow. Consider yourself lucky." Jeannie waved her hand toward the rest of the photographers. "None of us can seem to find any rest at all."

Devon went still. That sounded too familiar. She turned to face her coworkers. "None of you are sleeping?"

George ran his hand across his balding pate. "I close my eyes, but when I open them in the morning, I'm dragging." He glared down into his coffee cup. "I don't think I've loaded up on this much caffeine since I pulled all-nighters in college."

"Me, either," Jeannie said, stifling a wide yawn. It triggered yawns from everyone in the room.

Everyone except Devon.

"God, I envy you." Jeannie patted her on the shoulder and started heading to the conference room. "Come on. Time for the big meeting."

"Right," Devon said. She checked her pockets. What was she missing?

"I swear we go through this every two years," George said as he walked past with his oversized coffee mug.

Devon fell into step beside him. "Darn. Do you have a pen I could borrow?"

He sighed but pulled one out of his shirt pocket. "You'd better get your game together, kid."

"Yeah, yeah," Devon said as she walked through the conference room doorway. "I will."

As soon as she woke up.

She looked around to find a seat. The room was packed, and her favorite spot at the back was already taken. She looked toward the head of the table. There were a few chairs left up front, but she didn't want to sit up there right by—

"Ow!" Jeannie yelped.

Devon had stopped so suddenly, her coworker had plowed right into her. Jeannie's toe hit her heel, and her forehead bumped against her shoulder. Reaching up, Jeannie rubbed her head. "Don't stop like that."

Devon couldn't even get a decent apology out of her mouth. She stood there deaf, dumb, and mute as she gaped at the man sitting in their former boss's chair.

George gave her a none-too-gentle nudge. "Stop acting so weird in front of the new boss, kid."

This had to be some kind of bad joke—because if it wasn't she'd just officially gone over the edge.

The man sitting at the head of the table was her dream man!

"All right. If you're not going to take that seat, I will," George said as he waddled past.

Devon couldn't stop staring.

"Shall we get started?" her new boss asked.

He sounded like her dream man, too.

"Would you like to take a seat, Ms. Bradshaw?" he asked. "There's one up here."

He was looking at her with her dream man's dark, midnight eyes. Eyes full of lust . . . Eyes full of need . . . Oh, God. Devon wanted to melt right through the floor. Instead, she felt someone behind her give her a soft kick to the calf.

The only seat left was right next to him. She walked stiffly to the front of the room and sat.

What was happening? Was she still sleeping? Was this some kind of new, twisted nightmare?

She felt her new boss staring at her, and she glanced up. Their gazes locked. "Good morning," she said huskily.

Something sparked in his eyes. "Good morning."

Concentrating hard, she opened her notepad and readied her pen. That was something she'd never heard her dream man say before.

"Welcome, everyone."

His voice rumbled across her skin. That was her dream man's voice, all right. She'd heard it enough times; talking to her, whispering in her ear, yelling out when he . . .

God, what was going on?

"I think I introduced myself to everyone as I walked around earlier this morning, but if I missed you, my name is Cael Oneiros. I'm taking over for Tommy Bearing. From what I've heard, I've got big shoes to fill."

Devon shakily wrote "Cael Oniros" down on her notepad. *Cael.*

She rubbed a hand over her face as she felt it heat. She suddenly realized she'd never stopped to ask her midnight lover his name.

"That's Oneiros with a long *o* and a long *i*."

She started when he reached over and corrected the way she'd spelled his last name. Worse, his hand brushed against hers as he drew back. The incidental touch jarred Devon with its familiarity. His skin was taut, and his hand was warm. She felt her nipples tighten.

Her belly suddenly flared, the signal white hot. Startled, she caught it with the palm of her hand. Was this really happening? Had her dream lover just come to life?

"Am I awake?" she whispered to Jeannie.

The scowl hadn't left her coworker's face. "You tell me," she said dryly as she reached up to rub her sore head.

"I'm serious," Devon hissed. "Am I awake?"

Jeannie's forehead furrowed. "Yes. What's wrong with you?"

"I don't know." She was awake and sitting next to a man she didn't think existed. Her dream world had just crashed into reality—and it was one hell of a wreck.

God, she was gorgeous, Cael thought. He knew he was staring, but that was a lot safer than what he really wanted to do. He'd always thought she was beautiful, but in the sunshine, her auburn hair looked as if it had been licked by fire. Her eyes were greener, her lips pinker. But her skin was too pale—she looked as if she'd seen a ghost.

He shifted in his chair. He'd tried to catch her before the meeting but hadn't been able to find her. She must be feeling ambushed, but what could he have done to prepare her? Warn her that he wasn't just a figment of her imagination? He couldn't tell her what he really was.

"Uh, Mr. Oneiros?"

He looked at the portly, balding man who happened to be another one of his charges. George was waiting for him to speak, to say something inspiring. He looked around the room and felt the weight of his staff's combined stares.

Hell. He raked a hand through his hair.

"I realize that change isn't easy," he said, trying to remember his planned speech. He glanced at Devon out of the corner of his eye. "But I'm hoping that you'll all be open to new ideas."

New ideas like he was a real man and there might be a chance for a real relationship between them. She sat there so still, so distant. Wasn't she at all happy to see him? Wasn't she just the least bit intrigued?

"I want to assure you all that we'll ease into this transition. We'll figure out things as we go along. I know that this is a stressful time for everyone."

She was still staring blindly at his name on the notepad. God, what he'd give to be able to read her thoughts right now.

Looking down, he tried to concentrate on his notes. This was not how he'd planned things to go. He'd accepted this job offer more than a month ago. It was a good opportunity, but the deciding factor had been *her*. He'd wanted to meet her. He'd wanted his shot.

If she hadn't done that love spell, there wouldn't be a problem. She wouldn't even know who he was right now.

Frustrated, he tossed his pen onto the table. It hit with a clatter and he saw her jump.

"I've taken some time to review your past issues," he said, focusing on the task at hand, "and you're doing a lot of good things. I've seen some excellent stories and some outstanding photo work. I do think there's room for improvement, but that's a topic for a future discussion."

He sat a little straighter. "Right now, I realize that everyone is fighting just to keep up. We'll have to be in reactive mode until this spate of tragic events is over. Until then, strive for quality as we try to meet the quantity."

The words were coming out of his mouth, but all his attention was still on Devon. He wanted to shake her up, to make her respond to him. An idea popped into his head, and he went with it. "Jeannie, that picture you took this morning of the mayor is a perfect example of what I'm looking for."

Devon's head popped up so fast, it was a wonder she didn't give herself whiplash.

Jeannie blushed. "Thank you, sir."

Devon did a snap turn toward her colleague. "The mayor?"

Jeannie shrugged. "I happened to see him in the park as I was driving to work. It looked like he'd slept there."

"On a bench with a newspaper for a pillow?"

"Yeah," Jeannie said, her brow furrowing. "I didn't think you got here early enough to see the photo."

Devon sat motionless, but time started to almost pulse. Cael waited as her head slowly turned. When she finally looked at him, he felt the punch of desire hit him square in the gut.

"That was a money shot if I've ever seen one," he said quietly.

Her eyes went wide. He saw her muscles clench, but when she tried to push herself away from the table, he impulsively hooked his leg around the back of hers. It stopped her cold. He watched steadily as her cheeks flared red and her green gaze took on a confused, yet intimate glow.

She couldn't ignore him anymore. She couldn't pretend he wasn't there.

Cael felt his cock harden and was happy for the huge conference table that hid him. Spell or not, he liked that she knew who he was, even if she didn't know *what* he was.

"Uh, Mr. Oneiros?" George said.

"Yes?" he said absently.

"Today's assignments?"

"Right." He shook his head and sat back. "The assignments . . ."

Devon was fighting for every breath she took. There was no way this man could know about her dream. Absolutely no way. It was a coincidence; it had to be.

She gripped the arms of her chair tightly. She couldn't fathom the alternative. If he knew about her dream, then he also knew about the others . . . the things they'd done together . . . the things he'd done to her . . . She squeezed her legs together tightly when she remembered the way she'd ridden him on that park bench.

It didn't help. Her body couldn't separate the real man from the fantasy. All it remembered were his touches, his kisses, and his sensual demands. Sitting here beside him with all these people around was pure torture. Feeling his heat . . . Smelling his scent . . .

"Don't you want it, Devon?" he asked.

Startled, she looked at him. *"What?"*

"The 'Beat the Heat' assignment." He turned toward her. "I'm thinking pool shots, kids eating snow cones, that kind of thing. I know you had a tough assignment yesterday on the freeway. I thought you might like a break."

Her throat nearly closed off. "That's fine," she whispered.

She stared at his tie. Anyone would have been stressed out by the accident scene yesterday. It wasn't because she'd told him about it. It had nothing to do with last night's dream.

None of this did.

Taking a calming breath, she tried looking at him detachedly. There had to be a rational explanation for this. Maybe she had everything backward. If she was dreaming about him, she must have seen him somewhere before. He'd worked at a magazine; had they met at an industry dinner? An awards ceremony?

No, if she'd met this guy before, she would have remembered!

"George, I'd like you to take the Collingwood trial. Be careful; I've heard the protestors outside the courthouse are getting unruly."

"Yes, sir. I'm on it."

Devon went still. There was one other option. Seven months of a recurring dream had led her to do a lot of research. One of the more out-there scenarios was something called reciprocal dreams.

Shared dreams.

But that was getting into some weird stuff.

Magical stuff.

Her stomach thudded somewhere down near her toes. What had she done with that spell?

"That's it, everyone," Cael said. "Be careful out there, and let's make this first issue together a great one."

Devon hesitantly pushed back from the table. She looked at her new boss.

He watched her back, his eyelids heavy. "We need to talk later."

Her mouth went dry. "Later," she agreed.

Trying to act normal, she blended in with the moving crowd and headed back to her desk.

"Good meeting, huh?" George said as he strolled into their work bay. "Short and sweet. He seems like a decent guy."

"Huh," Devon mumbled. Opening the bottom drawer, she unzipped her purse. She grabbed her cell phone at the same time she remembered that it wasn't working. "Damn!"

Her fingers suddenly tingled.

She watched in disbelief as the screen flickered back to life.

Turning on her heel, she went to the hallway for some privacy. Her finger shook as she hit speed dial. She couldn't remember the last time she'd felt this stressed. One more heated twinge in her belly and she was going to snap like an overstretched rubber band.

"Hello?"

"Tasha!"

"Devon? What's wrong? You sound strange."

Not as strange as her friend sounded. Tasha was so tired, she sounded old. It threw Devon for a second and she almost reconsidered, but she couldn't keep this from her best friend. Tasha was the only person who could help her figure this out. She was the only one who'd understand. "Something weird just happened."

"Where are you?"

"I'm at work."

Tasha sighed, bringing back the image of fragility. "Honey, I told you. You can't keep taking pictures of those gruesome things and not have it affect you."

"It's not that. I'm still at the office." Devon gripped the phone tighter. "He's here!"

"Who's here?"

"My dream man."

The sound that Tasha let out was as jealous as it was disgusted. "You fell asleep at work? That is *so* not fair!"

"No. Listen to me!" Frustration made Devon talk too loudly. She dropped her voice and moved farther away from the photography bay. "I just met him in real life. My dream man is my new boss!"

Tasha went silent for a long time. "Are you sure?"

She'd never been more sure of anything in her life. He looked the same. He sounded the same. He even smelled the same. Oh God, he had that clean, masculine scent that drove her nuts.

"I think he knows about my dreams," she whispered, looking around. "He said things . . . I think we might have shared them."

"But that's . . . that's . . ."

"Impossible, I know—but it's happening!"

"I knew those dreams weren't good," Tasha said, her voice going hard. "Stay away from him. Get out of there."

"No, I don't think he's here to hurt me. I got a good—"

"You don't know what he'll do. You don't know what he is! That damn spell!"

"Tasha."

"We have to go back," her friend said decisively. "Back to see the witch doctor who started all of this. We need to end it."

Eleven

Tasha slammed down the phone and drummed her fingernails on the kitchen counter. She didn't want to wait until Devon took her pictures. She wanted to go back to the greenhouse now!

Not even the thought of seeing that stooped old herbalist was going to stop her. Still, the memory of his gnarled fingers and watery eyes made her uneasy. Briskly, she rubbed her arms. It didn't matter how scary he was; they needed to talk to him. Devon was the one who normally got special feelings about things, but this time *she* had a sinking feeling in her gut.

"This is not good," she said out loud. "Not good. Not good. Not good."

How could a dream become reality like this? Dev

had been seeing this man in her sleep for months and, out of the blue, he shows up as her new boss?

No way.

Something was wrong. Terribly, terribly wrong.

She ran a hand through her tousled hair, and her gaze darted around the kitchen. That old man had warned them to be careful with the spell, and they'd followed every instruction to a T. How could they have screwed it up? What did this dream man's appearance mean?

God, she couldn't think!

Rubbing her eyes, she walked into the living room. When she opened them again, splotches of red covered everything. She shook her head and her vision cleared. It only made her sketches pop out even more. They were spread everywhere. The living room sofa, the coffee table, the floor . . . One was even draped across her stereo.

"Ahhhh!" She couldn't look at them anymore. She'd been drawing as fast as she could, but everything that was coming out of her was dark and twisted. Unable to be around the sketches, she ended up in her bedroom. Not even bothering to lift her feet onto the bed, she collapsed backward onto the mattress.

Take the utmost care, the old man had warned. She'd thought they had!

"Earth, Water, Wind, and Fire, lead me to my heart's desire," she said softly. What was wrong with that?

A soft sound rumbled from somewhere near her headboard. Rolling her head, she looked at the wall that separated her apartment from Jason's. He'd come home a while ago; she'd heard him. Was he sleeping already?

Her body shifted on the bed, envious. The last good sleep she'd gotten was with him—and the last good sex. Her toes curled. That romp in the paint had been hot. And the best part was that a big O had finally let her sleep.

"Not fair," she said when she heard him again.

Her gaze went back to the ceiling. This thing with Devon had her worried. What could they have done wrong? Should they not have asked for the cardamom oil? Had that mandrake poisoned the mix? What could make a dream lover real?

"Bring passion, love, and romance before the waxing moon has passed." It didn't sound dangerous.

The noise on the other side of the wall became a definite grumble, and Tasha rolled over with a huff. Lust was one of the most powerful feelings trying to rule her, and each time she heard him, it became stronger and hungrier.

But she was *not* going over there. He was just too damn enticing, him and his pills. She knew he hadn't dropped that subject. Worse, she was getting more and more tempted to give in.

But she couldn't! Not when she had so little control.

"Why can't I just sleep?"

The rumble was suddenly interrupted by a snort, and she sat up in bed like a jack-in-the-box. Was he snoring?

Real or imagined, it didn't matter. All she knew he was over there sleeping. *Without her.*

Lust swelled within her and her energy came back. "Hmm," she hummed, her brain churning.

She marched to her closet, where she found her red four-inch stiletto heels. "These should do nicely."

She stepped into the ankle breakers and determinedly walked down the hallway. One eyebrow lifted as she arrived in her kitchen. She took a step inside. The clip-clop was like music to her ears.

"Ah yes, the music," she said, remembering his complaint. Opening her mouth, she started to sing. Loudly.

"If I can't sleep, then you're not going to sleep," she sang, making up the words. She walked around her kitchen, taking care to make every step echo. "Snore, you boor, and I'll sing some more."

She kept at it until she heard heavy footsteps on the other side of the wall. Excitement prickled inside her chest.

She followed the footsteps to what had to be his front door. It slammed shut, and her nerves twittered as the stomping came closer. Even knowing it was coming, she still jumped when he began pounding on her door.

"Open up, Tasha."

Adrenaline poured through her veins, readying her. When she pulled the door open, Jason stood with his arm propped against her door frame, looking studly and perturbed.

"What the hell are you doing?" he asked, his blue eyes flashing. His hot gaze ran over her from head to toe and stuck on her shoes. One eyebrow rose. "I thought we were going to try to be considerate of each other."

"That's what I thought, too," she said indignantly. "Could you be any louder?"

"*Me*? I was sleeping," he said, leaning closer to her. "You were the one caterwauling."

She poked him in the chest. "You were *snoring*."

"Ow," he said, pulling back. Reaching up, he rubbed the spot.

She watched, entranced, as his hand went round and round against his hot, muscled, lickable chest.

"And snorting," she said, poking his other pec.

"Ouch! Damn it." He moved fast. Before she knew it, he'd put his brawny shoulder into her stomach and picked her up. His hand connected with her bottom in a sharp swat. "Stop that."

"Ow!" she cried. "Put me down."

"So you can poke me again? I don't think so."

Hanging upside down, she found an even more tempting target. Eyes narrowing, she directed her finger toward his tight butt.

"Ow!" He lurched so hard, he nearly threw her over his shoulder. "God damn it, woman!"

"How can you sleep so easily?" She'd never been so jealous of someone in her life. "How, how, how?"

She was doubling her attack now, poking with both forefingers. And it was a sight to behold. Watching his ass clench was as fun as it was sexy.

"*Ah!*" He jumped, jostling her.

"Oof!" The air went out of her lungs as his shoulder caught her right in the diaphragm.

As she went limp, he used the opportunity to kick her door shut. "You are going to regret this."

Carrying her like a sack of potatoes, he headed down the hallway. It made it even harder for her to breathe. Each step he took squeezed the air right out of her lungs. She was gasping for oxygen when he tossed her onto the bed. She bounced, but he was on top of her before she could scramble away.

Tasha looked up. He'd caught her wrists in his hands and was crouching over her. His knees dug into the outside of her thighs, and his body was primed for any move she might make. It was the glitter in his blue eyes, though, that made her stay put.

Her stomach fluttered when his head dipped.

"Now I get to do the poking," he said, his voice low and raspy.

The bedroom whirled as he flipped her over. He pulled her hips back and up, and Tasha gasped as her nipples raked hard against the sheet. Excitement shot through her veins when he flicked up the hem of her nightshirt.

"Ahhh!"

She squealed with surprise when he poked her left cheek. That wasn't the kind of poke she'd been expecting. Her butt clenched just like she'd seen his do, but between her legs, heat exploded. Another poke to the right side of her ass and she got wet.

"Ooooo, Jason!" She tried to squirm away from his stimulating touch, but he hooked an arm around her and began tugging at her panties. They slid over her hips, and she groaned when his thumb trailed through her wet crease.

He leaned over her and nipped her ear. "I'll make you sing, baby."

He yanked her panties down farther and she twisted her legs, trying to help. The stretchy lace got as far as her stilettos before tangling around one of her heels. Desperately, she tried to toe off her shoe.

"Leave them on." His hands slid up her back, pushing her nightshirt up. "They're making me hard."

Tasha undulated underneath him. He'd pushed her shirt up over her head so she couldn't see. It only intensified her other senses. She could feel his heat against her back, her bottom, and the backs of her thighs.

She whipped the T-shirt off and looked over her shoulder.

Her arousal peaked when she saw the way he was

looking at her butt. He watched intently as he rubbed the globes round and round. When his thumbs dipped into her crease, her back arched sharply.

"Jason," she gasped as his thumbs rubbed across the bud of her anus.

She shuddered when he rubbed her pussy lips. He did it again, this time more firmly, and her head dropped onto the pillow as he spread her open wide.

"Oh, God," she groaned.

One of his hands suddenly left her, but the other began to play more intimately. She squirmed when one of his fingers penetrated her. From its strength and the thickness, she realized it was his thumb. Her entire body began to rock when he swirled it round and round.

"Why didn't you just ask me over?" he asked, his voice rough.

She heard the sound of his boxers coming off.

She bucked backward, impaling herself on that intrusive thumb. "Ayeeee," she gasped. "The sleeping pills. I knew you'd—"

He poked her again, and she nearly came.

"I don't . . . like . . . doctors," she managed to get out.

"I'm not a doctor."

But he liked playing one, she thought as her hips rolled. He'd added his fingers to the mix; they were tickling her clit as his thumb plunged and retreated.

"You know what I mean," she said, throwing a fierce look over her shoulder.

He caught her by the back of the neck. "But you like me?"

Her heart rolled over in her chest. "Yes," she whispered.

She liked him a lot.

He leaned over and kissed her hard. "Good. Because I can't get you out of my head."

He took his thumb out of her and wrapped his arm firmly around her hips. Positioning himself, he thrust his heavy cock into her.

"Oh!"

Tasha shuddered as he went deep. Melting, she turned and pressed her forehead into the pillow. God, he felt like he was tunneling right up into the heart of her.

"Damn, you feel good," he said. He brushed her hair to the side and began kissing the back of her neck.

"Mmm, Jason." She sighed as he began thrusting into her with long, silky strokes. "Put me to sleep again."

His hips twitched, his cock buried at the deepest point. "You really know how to pump up a man's ego, darlin'."

"I'll pump up whatever you need." Taking one arm from around the pillow, she reached between her legs.

She loved the way he grunted when her fingers began caressing his hard balls. "Just fuck me unconscious."

His grip on her tightened. "Whatever you need, baby."

His hips increased their pace, and Tasha cried out.

They felt incredible together. She could practically see a halo of pleasure shimmering around their joined bodies.

"Harder," she begged, pressing back with her hips.

He leaned over her again, and one hand went to her breast to pluck at her stiff nipple. "You are something else, little Whirlwind."

So was he. All blond heat and caring, muscled male.

She craned her head back, and he nipped at her neck.

Tasha gasped as her pussy clenched. The friction between their bodies escalated and each stroke fanned the fire inside her, hotter and hotter, higher and higher. He took her upward until she flew right over the top.

She cried out as pleasure streaked through her.

"Sleep, baby," he whispered.

Gladly. Headlong, she flew into that dark, comforting abyss.

Devon arrived at the greenhouse early. Finding a spot of shade away from the midday sun, she waited for

Tasha to arrive. Sweltering ninety-degree heat had put her nerves on edge. Swimming pools and snow cones? Why did he have to give her that assignment when she needed action?

Why was he doing this to her at all?

She still couldn't believe her dream man had shown up like that!

Nervously, she tugged at the belt loop of her denim skirt. If Tasha didn't show up soon, she was going to have to go into that greenhouse alone.

Out of the corner of her eye, Devon saw a red blur fly across the parking lot. Tasha was right on time, although she would have preferred her friend drive more slowly and be a little late. As tired as she'd been, her reflexes couldn't be that sharp.

"Hey," she called as Tasha hopped out of her sports car. She eyed her critically as she hurried toward her. In those red short shorts and sporty sunglasses, Tasha looked ready to take on the world. Only a close look at her face showed that she was still battling insomnia. The fatigue lining her forehead couldn't be covered with makeup.

"How are you feeling?"

As tired as Tasha looked, she seemed calm. "Nice. Jason came over, and I managed to get some sleep."

At once, Devon felt guilty. "You were sleeping? You shouldn't have gotten up! I could have done this alone."

"No, you couldn't have."

Devon bit her lip. Tasha knew her way too well.

"Did the nap help?" she asked. "Do you think you'll sleep tonight?"

"With Jason working? No." Tasha lifted her sunglasses and squinted as if the sunlight hurt her eyes. "I don't really know if these catnaps help at all. It's more like a mean tease."

Devon folded her arms over her chest. This was getting serious. "Don't you think it's time you considered his idea? Why not take the sleeping pills if he's there to watch you? He could act as your dispensary."

"No. He's not always there. He works nights, and I would find those pills. Believe me." Moving to the greenhouse's door, Tasha pulled it open and stepped inside.

Apparently that was the end of that discussion.

Devon took a deep breath. She really had no other resort than to consult with this guy. Summoning her nerve, she followed her friend inside.

The greenhouse was eerily vacant.

"How do they stay in business?" she whispered.

Tasha stood looking down the aisle toward the wooden door. The toe of her red stiletto tapped against the ground nervously. "Ready?"

"As ready as I'll ever be," she said, fighting back her apprehension.

They started toward the ivy-covered door. When they finally got there, Tasha reached out and gripped the handle. She stood frozen for a moment, but then straightened her spine and entered.

Devon followed, jumping when the heavy door smacked shut behind them.

It took a moment for her eyes to adjust to the dimness. When they did, she saw the herbalist hanging dried flowers from an overhead hook. He looked over his shoulder, and his watery blue eyes narrowed when he recognized the two of them.

"Why are you back?" he asked abruptly. "What have you done?"

Tasha flinched. Devon immediately took a step forward to stand by her side.

"That's what we need you to tell us," she said. "We did the spell. We were careful, but strange things have been happening ever since."

"I warned you not to trifle!" The old man's wrinkled face darkened, and he shook his head. He reached out for the table. Using it as a crutch, he hobbled over to his stool. "What has happened?"

Devon shared a glance with Tasha, who nodded.

"My dreams are starting to become real," Devon said. There it was, right out in the open.

Yet the old man didn't react.

Instead, he turned his haunting gaze on Tasha. "And you don't feel well."

Even in the dim light of the shed, Devon saw her friend pale. "You think it has something to do with the spell?" Tasha asked.

"It matters not," he said, waving his hand as he dismissed the subject. "Tell me exactly what you did."

Tasha immediately reached into her purse. She pulled out the wrinkled piece of paper on which the spell was written. Smoothing it, she set it on his table and stepped backward.

Devon waited with bated breath as the man read the ritual. When he lifted his head, he looked straight at her.

"Tell me of these dreams."

She licked her dry lips. "I've had a recurring dream for several months. In it, there's a man. Today he showed up as my new boss—and he knows things." Her voice dropped. "Things he shouldn't know."

"Is he your heart's desire?"

She blushed. This was way too personal to share with a complete stranger. "In a way."

The herbalist's eyes narrowed astutely. She suspected that he understood a lot more than he was letting on.

"What powers do you possess?" he asked.

"What do you mean?"

"Do you not have special abilities?" He waved his gnarled hand in a circle. "I saw your talents when you first visited me, and I see them now—only the colors are more vibrant. Vibrant and chaotic, with splotches here and there. It's all jumbled."

Tasha's elbow connected with her side. "Tell him about 'it.'"

Devon went still. She didn't know if she was comfortable with that.

"*It*," the old man said, snapping his fingers to get their attention. "What is this 'it'?"

"She knows things before they happen," Tasha said, answering for her.

"Visions?"

She shook her head. "Feelings." She pointed at Devon's belly. "Right here. Gut feelings. Good or bad, they always come true."

Devon felt the old man's gaze turn on her. "You have the gift of foresight. These things you're feeling are premonitions."

Put that way, it didn't sound so bad. Or so crazy. Her dreams could have just been premonitions that she'd meet Cael.

She liked that answer a lot.

Just as she was getting used to it, though, the herbalist made a tsking sound. "There is one other possibility." He pushed the paper away and leaned both hands on the table. "You may have conjured him."

Devon felt the air in the shed get heavier, more ominous. The word had the hint of evil to it. It sent a chill right through her, despite the temperature outside.

"Conjured," Tasha repeated. Her fingers curled around the shoulder strap of her purse. "Black magic? We summoned him? But it was such a simple spell. How could we have done that?"

For once, it was the old man who looked confused. "Your friend *is* a powerful witch."

"A witch?" Devon gasped.

Tasha of glanced sharply at Devon. "She is not."

He shrugged. "Think what you must, but she is a witch."

Devon wanted to deny the accusation, but all she could think about were the colors that had flown from her fingertips the other night. And her cell phone. And the wineglass. She looked down at her hands. It couldn't be. There was no such thing as a witch. Not a real one.

Still, her inner sense was jangling. It was that uncertain tingle again.

Her jaw suddenly dropped. "He knows."

"Who knows?" Tasha asked.

"My dream man. Cael." Suddenly, the mingling scents of the herbs were overpowering. They filled her head . . . her chest . . . "He asked me about this last night when I slept! I just didn't know what he was talking about."

"He was plying you for information?" Tasha's eyes hardened. All fear left her, and she walked right up to the herbalist's table and knocked on it with her knuckles. "This conjuring thing. How do we get rid of him? How do we cancel the spell?"

The old man looked down at the paper. "Have you met your heart's desire?"

She shrugged. "I don't know. Maybe. Why?"

"Then the spell worked. It's served its purpose."

She shook her head, refusing to accept his answer. "Then how do we reverse it?"

The old man pointed his gnarled finger at the two of them. "You will not mess with these matters again."

"She conjured someone. Some*thing*," Tasha said, slapping her hand down sharply. "Something evil has been probing around in her head for months. That spell opened the door and let it in. We have to send it back!"

Devon quickly stepped forward and put her hand on Tasha's shoulder. She looked at the old man, meeting his gaze steadily. "What should I do?"

He let out a ragged breath. "It could be nothing. Learn more about him, but be careful."

"And what about me?" Tasha asked, her voice cracking. "What do I do?"

The old man's hawklike features softened. He tottered around the table and grabbed a glass container off a lower shelf. Turning, he placed it in her hands. "Drink this tea. It has valerian and will help you sleep."

Tasha looked at the herbalist incredulously. "How did you know?"

He waved his hand in an all-too-familiar circle. "Your aura." He sighed heavily. "Little one, it's *your* future that worries me the most."

Twelve

Cael stared down at the article in front of him, not really seeing it. He'd read the first paragraph three times, but it had yet to sink in. Swearing softly, he glanced up and looked out his open office door.

Devon wasn't back yet.

He glanced at his watch. She'd left to do that fluff piece he'd assigned her a while ago. Was she ever coming back?

As if the first day at a new job wasn't stressful enough.

Reaching up, he rubbed the back of his neck. He needed to concentrate. Woman problems or not, he had a job to do—and that meant getting tomorrow's issue in the can. He skimmed the article in front of him one more time. They had plenty of good stories. The day had been so crazy, choosing the headline story would be the tough part.

And actually, this one had potential.

The reporter was young, but he'd scooped the rest of the staff. Apparently the mayor's office had more problems than just the city leader spending the night on a park bench. His interest piqued, Cael picked up his blue pencil. The piece was well written, and it had two reliable sources backing it up. He made a few notes in the margin. Just a bit of tweaking and this was going on the front page.

As he edited, though, familiar names started popping out at him. Mary Phillips, Johann VanSteeg, Sammy Steele, Tina Mills . . . An uneasy feeling settled in his stomach. Quickly, he flipped through the stack of papers to the next story. Rory James, Lani Mortensen . . .

His chair skidded backward as he stood up quickly. He brushed more paper aside. Carl Xavier, Nancy Lloyd . . .

"Fuck," he breathed, his chest tight. He ran both hands through his hair. They were all his charges!

"Fuck!" He knew he'd missed them a few times— maybe quite a few times—but enough to cause reckless driving and assault?

He glanced down at his desk. "Indecent exposure, Carl? Really?"

"Mr. Oneiros?"

He jerked and spun around. His new secretary, Lois, stood in the doorway. She seemed competent enough, but he was already picking up signs that she preferred getting her news through sub-channels. Mainly the grapevine.

"Need something, Lois?"

"John is wondering about his story."

Cael nodded, even though his heart was about to burst right out of his chest. Stiffly, he picked up the draft. "Tell him to make these changes and run with it. It's going on the front page under the fold."

Lois's eyes were a little too bright for his liking. "Yes, sir," she said.

As she left, a flash of auburn hair caught his attention. His pulse jumped even higher. "Devon," he called.

She headed to her desk and disappeared from sight.

Cael glanced down at the troubling information on his desk. Which problem did he tackle first? He glanced up. No question: the pretty one.

Trying not to be too obvious, he strode out of his office. The click of keyboards and random chatter hit his ears. Walking through the bustle, he nodded whenever one of his new staff members caught his eye. When he stopped in the doorway to the photography room, Devon didn't notice him. Taking the opportunity, he took a moment to watch her.

She was intent on her work, pulling up the digital pictures she'd taken that day. As he'd asked, she'd captured lots of happy kids and smiling faces. He hoped those would provide a good contrast to the rest of the tragedy they had to report.

And speaking of doom . . .

"Devon," he said quietly.

She spun around on her chair. "Oh! Cael . . . I mean, Mr. Oneiros."

Even with dozens of people around, he felt himself harden. It was the first time she'd ever called him by his name. "Cael is fine," he said gruffly.

She was nervous. She'd crossed her legs, and her top foot was starting to bounce. The motion only drew his attention to the amount of skin that short skirt bared. She had great legs—long, sleek, and sexy. He folded his arms across his chest to stop himself before he did something stupid.

"I . . . I'm sorry I didn't get back sooner." She pushed back her hair, and his fingers itched. "I've got the photos right here."

She spun back to her monitor and clicked the mouse.

"As I was driving in, I also saw a Little League mom taking out her frustrations on a minivan." The pointer on the screen jiggled a little. Cael moved closer, and he heard her inhale sharply. He did the same and smelled her subtle perfume.

"Think we can use it?" she asked, pointing at the

picture of the woman swinging a baseball bat at a windshield.

He looked at the screen, then did a double take. Caroline Shaw. Shit, things were getting out of control. His mind raced as he considered what he should do.

One thing at a time.

"Can I see you in my office, Devon?"

She looked up at him sharply, and her face paled.

He barely stopped himself from reaching out to brush her cheek and instead took a step back. "It's time for that talk."

She wanted to say no, he could see it. Gripping the back of her chair, he rolled her away from her computer.

"But the pictures . . ."

"You've got plenty of time before the deadline." Turning, he headed toward his office. There were some pluses to being the boss. At night in private, he never knew what she was going to do. Here, she had to follow him.

Together, they walked back through the newsroom. One or two reporters threw them questioning looks, but a squawk from the police scanner soon diverted their attention. Cael waved Devon ahead of him into his office. Uneasiness filled her eyes when he closed the door behind them.

"Have a seat," he said as soothingly as he could.

He watched as her gaze snapped from him to the door and back again.

"I'm sorry I was late this morning," she said. "I overslept."

Because she'd had a really good night, he thought. They both had. He shoved his hands into the front pockets of his pants.

"That's not why I asked you here." He hated that she was this suspicious of him. "We never had a chance to talk this morning, and you seemed . . . upset by my appointment."

"It wasn't your appointment."

She approached the chair he'd offered, but instead of sitting, she gripped its back. He didn't miss how white her fingers became. "Tommy had nothing but good things to say about you. I know you're very quali-fied. It's just . . ."

He waited. "Yes?"

She looked away. He saw the pulse at her temple flutter before she looked at him again. "Have we met before?"

Awareness suddenly filled the room. They both knew they had, but how could he answer her ques-tion? He doubted that the truth would make her feel any better about things. More likely, it would send her running toward the door.

And that was the absolute last thing he wanted.

Frustration burned inside Cael's chest. Yes, they'd

met before. They'd talked, they'd fought, and they'd had hot, raunchy sex until neither of them could move. They were lovers. They had a relationship. "You look familiar," he forced himself to say.

Her eyes sparked. "Where did you come from?"

"Come from?" Did she think he'd popped out of a pod or something?

She pushed back from the chair. "I mean what was your last job? Are you new in town?"

So she *was* curious about him. Funny how such a little thing could take so much weight off his shoulders. Casually, he leaned his hips back against his desk. He was curious about her, too. Hell, he was insatiable for every last detail he could learn. "I've worked at various newspapers and magazines, the last being *The Edge*. I transferred to Solstice to take over as the lifestyles editor there a little over seven months ago."

She looked at him quickly. "Seven months?"

He tensed. For some reason that was important. "Yes."

She was looking at him so intently, the air began to vibrate. "And how long ago did you accept the *Sentinel*'s offer?"

He wished he understood the direction of her questioning. He had the feeling that the way he answered could affect everything. "About a month ago," he answered carefully.

"So all *before*," she murmured more to herself than him. She looked down at her hands and gently flexed her fingers. When she realized he was watching, she nervously rubbed her palms against her skirt.

All he wanted to do was pull her into his arms and tell her everything was going to be all right. To kiss her and put all this uneasiness behind them. To make love to her and forget the world. "Anything else?" he asked.

"No," she said softly, then immediately changed her mind. Her chin came up determinedly, and she looked him directly in the eye. "How have you been sleeping?"

That was it. He couldn't take it anymore. "My nights have been out of this world."

Going with his gut, he pushed himself away from the desk. They'd never had problems communicating in the dream realm. She watched, wide eyed, as he walked toward her. He stopped barely inches from her and felt the magnetism between their bodies pull hard. Lifting his hand, he gave in to the need to touch her. Gently, he cupped the nape of her neck.

"Have dinner with me."

She went still. So still he could barely see her breathing.

He waited, his heart in his throat. "Just dinner," he said, letting his thumb brush against her soft skin.

She looked up at him, stunned. Her mouth parted, and her tongue darted out to wet her lips.

Then a sudden knock on the door had her springing back. Swearing under his breath, Cael planted his hands on his hips. "Yes?" he said sharply.

Lois poked her head in. "Sorry to interrupt."

She didn't come in, but she quickly evaluated the scene. Devon gave her nothing; she was already standing ten feet across the room. Lois cleared her throat. "The crowd that swarmed the courthouse this morning has re-formed down at the jail, but George is at a doctor's appointment. Would you like another photographer down there?"

She looked speculatively at Devon.

"I'm available," Devon said, already moving toward the door.

"No," Cael said.

Both women looked at him, one curious and one offended. Hell! He raked a hand through his hair. "I don't like it." For too many reasons. He let out a harsh breath. "How unstable is the situation?"

Lois shrugged. "We don't know, but John is already on his way to cover the story."

Devon plucked the note out of Lois's hand. "It's my job," she said, her green eyes flashing. "I can handle it."

He knew she could handle it; she was one of the best photographers on staff.

"Go," he said. "But be careful."

Cael showed up at the bar tired and grouchy. He had photographers and journalists still out, but the evening editor had come in. As tough as the day had been, he was happy with the way tomorrow's edition had come together.

Too bad he couldn't say as much about his love life.

He sat down heavily at a booth and signaled for the waitress. She brought a menu as Tony and Derek showed up.

"So how did it go?" Tony asked, sliding onto the seat. He shook his head when the waitress offered to bring more menus.

Cael loosened his tie. He really didn't know how to answer that question. He'd thought he'd started to get through to Devon, to make a connection with her, but then the daytime world had gotten in the way. "As well as I could have expected," he said.

"But not as well as you'd hoped," Derek surmised.

He tilted his head in acknowledgment.

Tony looked at the waitress, who was waiting patiently. "I'll have a burger and a Heineken."

Cael hadn't even realized the woman was still standing there. Tiredly, he passed the menu back. "I'll have the same."

"Make that three," Derek said. He spied a bowl of peanuts on the next table and swiped them.

"Give Red a little time," Tony said as the waitress left. "This has got to be coming as quite a shock to her. You're the one who told her she's been dreaming. Can you imagine going to work one day and finding you sitting there?"

Cael shifted uncomfortably. He didn't have to imagine it; he'd seen it with his own eyes. It hadn't been pretty. "I'll give her all the time she needs, but this whole thing has her pretty edgy."

"Ah, don't worry." Tony frowned at the way Derek was hogging the peanuts. Batting his hand away, he grabbed some for himself. "I saw how she reacted when I showed up at her bedside. She wanted you there."

He waved a peanut in Cael's direction. "Come on, admit it. You two have a good thing going in the dream realm. She's got to at least be curious."

"She's curious, all right," Cael said dryly. "About a lot of things."

"Things like what?"

They all looked up to see Mack sliding into the empty seat.

"You think I'd miss this?" he asked.

The waitress showed up with their drinks. When she saw Mack, she raised her eyebrows. "One more?"

He looked around the table. "What are we having?"

"Burgers and fries."

"Sounds good, but I'll take a Coke with that." He rubbed a hand over his face. "I just got up."

He watched their waitress go, clicking his tongue as he watched the sway of her hips. When she rounded the bar, he turned back to the discussion. "So am I too late? What did Sexy Red do when she saw you?"

Cael ran his thumb along the lip of the beer bottle. He was getting really tired of being the family entertainment. "She acted like she'd seen a ghost," he said grumpily.

Mack snagged a peanut from the fast-disappearing supply. "I guess we are kind of ghosts."

"It was a busy day, but I finally cornered her late this afternoon." Cael was still stewing over the way they'd been interrupted. Just an indication, some tiny hint, and he wouldn't be going out of his mind right now. "She started interrogating me like she was CIA."

"What did you say?" Derek asked.

Cael's jaw hardened. "What am I supposed to say? I dodged things as well as I could."

"Which probably made her even more skittish."

"Score one for the brainiac."

Tony set down his mug. The look on his face was sympathetic. "But the attraction was still there, right? That didn't just disappear."

No, it was stronger than ever. Cael stared into his beer as he remembered the way her pulse had fluttered in her temple. And how she'd licked her lips. *What had she been going to say?*

His brother grunted. "From the look on your face, that was the only thing that wasn't a problem."

It all depended on how you looked at it. Seeing Devon but not being able to touch her was pure torture. He picked up his coaster and tossed it onto the center of the table. "I just feel like we've gone back to square one."

"There's not much we can do to help you with that,"

Derek said. "But with any luck, now that you two have met, her interference in the dream world will end."

But he didn't want it to end. He wanted her in his arms. He wanted her in his bed. *Now.* Who knew how long it would be before he got her underneath him again?

Cael ran a hand over his face. Damn. He could feel that binding spell pulling at him even now.

"I actually called you here for another reason." Reaching into his back pocket, he pulled out the papers he'd copied. He unfolded them and tossed them onto the table. "Those are some of the stories you'll be seeing in tomorrow's paper. I noticed a common denominator in a lot of them."

Derek brushed the salt off his hands and picked up the articles. "I don't see anything," he said as he scanned them. "It's all a bunch of random violence and strange accidents—just like we've been seeing for the past few weeks."

Cael gestured with his beer. "Most of the names are mine."

Derek's brow furrowed. Tony reached out and took the bottom sheet. His eyes went back and forth as he read. "Wait. This one here—the guy who stripped down and plunged into the park fountain—he's mine."

"But Cael's right," Derek said, flipping to another sheet. "Most of them are his."

Cael hated to be the one not carrying his share of the load. "I'm falling behind more than I realized."

God, he wasn't used to asking for help. Taking a deep breath, he sat up a bit straighter. "I need to ask you guys to pick up the slack for me until I've got this situation with Devon straightened out. This spell she's got me under is unbreakable. I've tried, but I can't shake loose."

Mack looked up from the story he'd been trying to read upside down. "We already have, Cael. In fact, that's why I'm here. I need to talk to you about one of your charges."

"I can't do any more than I'm already doing," Tony said. "We may be an army of a thousand, but it's a big world."

"I know it's asking a lot," Cael said, trying to keep calm, "but this spell of hers has me trapped. Even when I try to avoid her, she comes after me."

"Are you sure that's the spell working?" Derek asked quietly.

Cael's irritation bubbled over. "I know what being a Dream Wreaker's all about, Derek. I'm not shirking my responsibilities."

"Aren't you? It seems to me if you wanted to break free, you could."

Mack suddenly leaned forward onto his elbows. "We've got company."

Their waitress returned with his Coke and another bowl of peanuts.

"Thanks," Cael said stiffly.

The woman glanced around the table, and her

friendly smile fell. No doubt she'd had enough experience with bar fights to sense one brewing. "Everything all right, boys?"

Cael stared stonily out the window while Derek brooded.

"They will be," Tony said.

One of her eyebrows lifted.

"I'll keep them in line," he promised.

She seemed skeptical but walked away, glancing over her shoulder to check on them.

Mack leaned toward the middle of the table again. "Pointing fingers isn't going to help," he hissed. "And I'm serious about your charge. I'm worried about her."

Cael couldn't shake his fighting mood. "Which one?" he asked, his glare still on Derek.

Mack snapped his fingers in front of his face, trying to get his attention. "That spunky little artist. The one with the long, dark hair and tiny, hot bod?"

Cael went still, his issues with Derek forgotten. "Tasha?"

"That's the one. God, she's a looker." Mack shook his head. "I've taken care of her a few times when she's fallen asleep during the day. She's dating one of my charges, but she's in bad shape. Her brain waves are all over the place. This morning it was so hard to catch one of her spindles, I nearly called one of you in to help me.

"When she finally took the dream, she sucked me

right in. I couldn't disconnect—and that was a freaky little nightmare she took me on. That sweet thing needs REM sleep like nobody's business. Cael, we're losing her. She's close to a total mental breakdown."

Cael felt sick. He didn't like the implications of this at all. "I've tried to catch her numerous times." And that was the God's honest truth. "But she's dealing with insomnia, too. I can't give her dreams if she's not sleeping."

Derek frowned. "Is this Tasha St. James?"

"That's the one," Mack said.

"I've seen her work. She needs to dream, Cael. She's really centered on her creative side."

Tony lifted his beer. "Hell, I'll take her," he offered. "If she's that hot, I'll make her my own personal— *Jesus!*"

A form had suddenly appeared at the end of their booth. Tony jumped back, and his shoulder slammed against the wall. Derek was so surprised, he dropped his peanuts. The form materialized in full. It was Devon.

Cael gaped right along with the rest of the people in the bar.

She looked around in panic. Her gaze rested on Tony first, and she only became more confused.

"Red!" Cael said sharply. He reached for her hand, and she finally saw him.

The look on her face was terrified.

"Help me!" she cried.

He felt her hand fading. He gripped tighter, but in a flash, she was gone.

Their waitress skidded to a stop and one of their burgers went flying. The plate smashed to the ground just as she let out a surprised scream.

The Oneiros brothers were already on the move. Mack scrambled out of the booth before Cael could storm right over him.

"What the fuck was that?" Tony barked as they rushed toward the door.

Derek threw some money onto the table. "She just astral projected."

Cael already had his car keys in his hand and was reaching for his cell phone to call the office. "And the worst part is that she's not sleeping."

Thirteen

Devon had blacked out for a moment, but she was right back in the middle of the nightmare she'd left. Only this was a living, breathing nightmare.

She was caught in a full-fledged riot.

The crowd pressed upon her and she couldn't get away. Sweaty bodies surrounded her, taking up her space.

Claustrophobia clawed inside her chest, and she went up onto her tiptoes to try to see where she was. An elbow jabbed her in the back. She was jostled from the side at the same time, and she fought to stay upright. "Stop pushing!"

"I'll push if I want, bitch," an angry woman

snarled. She put both hands on Devon's back and gave a heave.

Devon fell hard onto her knees. All she saw was a sea of legs and shuffling feet. She struggled to get up but couldn't find her footing. The crowd surged again, picking her up like an ocean wave. She was about to go under again when somebody wrapped an arm about her waist.

"Ahh!" she cried when she was yanked unceremoniously to her feet. She gulped in the clammy air. "Thank you. I—"

"No!" she screeched when her rescuer slid his other hand boldly under her skirt. He cupped her mound aggressively, and she instinctively kicked back with all her might.

Her sandals were flats, but the heels were hard. They connected with his shin, and he let out a howl. He let go of her fast. She whirled around, but the crowd swept her away before she could see who'd touched her so lewdly.

The hoard of people just didn't stop coming. Somebody tugged at her camera, and she pushed them away.

Frantically, she looked for a way out. She'd tried to stay out of the fracas. She'd kept to the edges. The crowd had been heading for the jail, but it had turned on a dime. It was almost as if people had forgotten about the Collingwood verdict entirely. They were now rioting for riot's sake. When they'd switched directions, she'd had no escape. She'd been caught up in the flow.

And now she was worried that she would be swallowed up whole.

"Let me out! Please, somebody help me!"

Darkness started narrowing her field of vision again, and she shook her head to clear it. She didn't know how she'd survived passing out on her feet the first time—or why she'd thought of her dream man. *He* couldn't help her.

"Oh, God," she whimpered. "Please get me out of this."

Jutting out her elbows, she started forcing her way through. Nobody else was being polite. Somebody stepped on her toe, and she yanked her foot back. Hobbling, she kept pushing forward. If she could just get to the edge of the crowd, she might be able to squeak out.

"Excuse me," she said. She stumbled when she got pushed again. She clutched her camera tightly to her body, but it left her with no way to defend herself when a big, hairy hand grabbed her breast.

The sound Devon let out was animalistic. Turning, she kicked at the man. It didn't even faze him; he just squeezed harder. With an angry cry, she tilted her camera upward and pressed the flash.

Even in the sunny evening, the bright light blinded him. He let out a curse and reached for his eyes. Devon fought to pull back, to get away, but there were no holes in the wall of people. She never even saw the backhand coming, but she felt it and saw stars.

"Hey!" a voice roared near her ear.

Suddenly, a fist went flying through her peripheral vision. Knuckles crunched against the degenerate's chin, and he crumpled.

"Get up, you ugly son of a bitch! If you want to hit someone, try hitting me!"

Devon thought she recognized her rescuer's voice, but it was too rough and angry for her to be sure. She was too woozy.

Strong hands suddenly caught her by the waist. "Hang on, Red," a deep voice said into her ear. "I've got you."

She didn't recognize that voice, but the man shielded her with his body protectively.

"Watch it, Cael!" he said.

The pervert came raging out of the crowd but walked directly into a right hook. He fell like a piece of lumber.

"Cael?" Devon pressed her hand to her sore cheek and looked over her shoulder.

Her muscles tensed. The man holding her upright was from her dreams, all right—only it was the one she'd seen nude! "You!"

To her amazement, red splotches appeared on his cheekbones.

"Yeah, me," he mumbled. He nudged her forward. "Your guy's over here."

Devon felt another pair of strong arms wrap around

her, and tears pressed at her eyes. She'd know her dream man's touch anywhere. Even being tossed about in the crowd, she recognized his scent and his heat. "You came."

"Of course I did," he said. A shuddering breath ruffled her hair.

"Here," he said, taking the camera that was jabbing into his chest. He lifted the strap over her head and passed it to another man. "Derek, take this."

He brushed a kiss across her temple. "Let's get out of here."

A group of men formed a protective circle around her. Cael wrapped an arm around her waist and tucked her close to his side as they began to bully their way out of the rioting crowd. Somehow, he'd shown up with a team of bodyguards. She was surrounded by four very capable men.

Still, it seemed like forever before they burst free. Devon inhaled the warm air deeply, savoring every bit of oxygen she could get. She'd thought she was going to be crushed.

Cael turned and pulled her against his chest, and their bodies sealed from head to toe. He tucked her head into the crook of his neck and murmured soft words into her ear. She hugged him back.

"Are you okay?" he asked.

She nodded but winced when her cheek rubbed against his chest. "Damn," she hissed. That bastard had gotten her good.

Cael gently ran his thumb across her cheekbone. It was tender, and she flinched. "I should have killed the son of a bitch," he said softly.

His buddies moved closer. One of them brushed his fingers across her temple. "At least he didn't break the skin. That would have been a shame."

She felt Cael inhale roughly.

So did she. His friends were good-looking, but she'd just escaped a mob. "Can I get some space, please?" she asked, unable to stop her voice from jumping.

"Oh, hell."

"What were we thinking?"

"Back off, guys."

Devon eased away from Cael's embrace. Self-consciously, she pushed her hair back from her face. With her clothes wrinkled, her hair wild, and a nice bruise forming, she must be quite the sight. "Are you going to introduce us?" she asked, hating how her voice wavered.

Cael ran a hand gently over her head. "Sure." Realizing how unsettled she was, he caught her hand. "Devon, these are my brothers."

"Your *brothers*?"

He nodded. "This is Derek and Mack."

Her mind flew in a dozen different directions as she mechanically reached out and shook their hands. "Thank you for saving me."

Both were tall, dark-haired, and so handsome it

wasn't fair. Those family genetics were something else. "Brothers," she said in amazement.

Cael looked at her in concern. "Are you sure you're okay?"

She waved her hand by her face. Most of all, she just felt stupid. She'd been running scared from him all day long because of what that nutcase at the greenhouse had told her. The herbalist had put that word "conjured" into her head, and she'd actually considered it. But she couldn't have conjured a whole family!

"And this is Tony," he said.

She paused as she faced her remaining rescuer. She'd definitely dreamed about this one. She bit her lower lip. He was big and muscled and just as attractive as the others. Still, he looked as self-conscious as she felt, shuffling from one foot to the other. Why would he be embarrassed?

Devon suddenly pressed a hand over her mouth. He knew about that dream!

"I'm glad to meet you," he said politely.

She mumbled something in return. Just how many dreams had she shared? And with how many people? She felt her adrenaline waning fast, and she leaned heavily against Cael. "Can we get out of here?"

He looked at her sharply. "Sure."

Mack surveyed the crowd. "We'd better move now. They're changing directions again."

Devon hesitated. "What about my car?"

"Where is it?" Tony asked.

"On Celestial Avenue."

He shook his head. "We'll never get to it from here. Do you have the keys?"

She patted her pockets and relaxed when she found them. Still, she hesitated about putting them into his uplifted palm. He was still a stranger to her.

"It's all right," Cael said. "They'll drop it off wherever you want."

Devon clutched her beagle keychain. "But my laptop and my purse are locked in the trunk."

Derek eyed the crowd critically. "If we're lucky, they'll still be there."

"Come on," Cael said as he escorted her down the block.

Devon suddenly remembered why she'd been there in the first place. "My photos!"

Derek held up her Canon, and she let out a sigh of relief. "I need to send them in."

"We'll do it. Don't worry." Cael took her keys and gave them to Tony as they stopped by a very nice black sedan. Reaching in his pocket, he pulled out his own keys. The locks clicked as he pressed the keyless entry, and he opened the passenger-side door for her.

Devon nearly groaned at the idea of sitting down and not getting crushed. When she stepped off the curb and settled onto the seat, though, she let out a gasp. Her knees burned like fire.

"Damn!" Cael said, dropping into a crouch.

"Oooh, that's got to sting," Mack said, bending over for a closer look.

Devon went still as Cael slid his hand up the back of her leg. He cupped her calf in his palm and gave her a soft squeeze. The intimate sensation kept going right up and settled between her legs. She bit her lip to keep from moaning.

He glanced up at her.

Their gazes locked, and she felt their connection all the way down to her soul. "How did you find me?" she whispered. "How did you know I needed you?"

He glanced over his shoulder, and his brothers got the message. One by one, they turned and headed for the car parked behind his. Derek opened the back door and deposited her camera before catching up with the rest.

Something inside Devon's chest fluttered when Cael looked at her again.

"I just knew," he said, his voice rough.

Heat unfurled in her belly. It didn't matter that she didn't understand what was happening between them. They had a bond that she couldn't deny. Maybe they had met the night she'd done that spell. Maybe they'd just met this morning. She didn't care. She cupped his face with both hands.

For such a big, tough guy, the gentle touch stopped him cold.

She leaned forward, and his dark eyes blazed. "Thank you," she whispered. She brushed her lips across his. He practically dragged her out of the car and into his embrace. He kissed her possessively, and she clutched him right back. They were both out of breath when he finally set her back on the seat.

"That's it, Sexy Red," he said softly. His dark eyes burned brighter than ever before. "I'm taking you home."

Her dream man was here. He'd rescued her. And the attraction Devon felt for him was overwhelming.

Everything suddenly seemed new and different. *This was real.* In all her dreams, she'd let her inhibitions go. Could the two of them really live up to their combined imaginations?

If their imaginations had really combined at all . . .

The way he drove straight to her house made her believe they had.

He parked in her driveway, and she automatically reached for her keys.

"Damn," he said, seeing the gesture.

"It's all right," she said. Getting out of the car, she looked around to make sure that nobody was watching. Deciding it was safe, she retrieved her backup key from the niche under the back steps. Her hand shook as she tried to push it into the lock.

"Let me get that," he said.

His hand closed over hers, and she let out a ragged breath.

"Relax," he said softly into her ear.

Devon shivered as his hot breath hit the side of her neck. Just how was she supposed to do that? She couldn't hide behind work anymore. She'd downloaded the pictures from her camera to her cell phone in the car to avoid talking to him. Then when she'd rallied her nerve, he'd called in to check on the reporters. There was no work left for them to do.

It was time to face what had been happening between them these past weeks.

She stepped inside her house, away from his disconcerting presence. He entered after her but immediately pushed her behind him when he heard a clicking sound coming from the kitchen.

Devon sighed in relief. "It's all right." She dropped to a squat. "Hey, boy."

Cael looked at the beagle in surprise. "You have a dog?"

"This is Cedric," Devon said, rubbing him firmly behind the ears. "I sort of share him with the neighbors."

She wanted to cuddle the friendly pooch and let him nuzzle all her fears away, but her knees were burning too badly. Gritting her teeth, she gave him one last scratch and pushed to her feet. She couldn't have been more surprised when he waddled past her to investigate their visitor.

She looked at Cael in surprise. Cedric was a sweet thing, but it usually took him a while to warm up to men. She watched as the dog sniffed the air, then began to wag his tail. "He acts like he recognizes you."

She couldn't see Cael's face as he leaned over to pet the dog. "Animals like me."

She wasn't buying it. She looked around the kitchen. He'd been here before—but only in her dreams. How could Cedric be sensing that?

Feeling off balance, she backed up until she could grip the counter. She went still when Cael straightened and glanced toward the table—the table where they'd made love. His hot gaze turned on her, and the clock ticked as they stared at each other.

"Let's take care of those knees," he said, his voice gruff.

Her stomach flipped. She wasn't ready for this. "They're not that bad," she lied.

He patted his hand on the counter next to the sink. "Humor me."

He turned toward her refrigerator, and Devon let out a puff of air. Suddenly, sitting down didn't seem like such a bad idea. Turning her back to the counter, she hitched herself up onto it. Her legs dangled over the side, and she tugged at her skirt, trying to get it to cover more skin. Heat flooded her face when he caught her.

"I'm thinking that a dress code of jeans and flannel shirts at the office might be a good idea," he said, walking back toward her.

The unexpected humor threw her.

"That's kind of unrealistic on a ninety-degree day, don't you think?"

He folded a bag of frozen peas in a dishcloth, then gently pressed it against her bruised cheekbone. "Yeah, I can see George being the sweaty type."

Devon reached up to hold the ice pack in place. Her fingers brushed against his, and the look he shot her was intimate.

It got even more intimate as he looked down at her red, scraped knees. Gently, he stroked the side of her leg. "Did that asshole do this to you, too?"

Shivers ran over her skin, making her toes clench. "No, somebody else pushed me."

His lips flattened. "I never should have let you go."

Anger rose up inside her. "It's what I do."

He stepped up to her, and her pulse jumped. "You were running from me."

She hesitated. It was the truth. "Do you know why?"

A muscle near his mouth jumped, but then he pulled back to grab a paper towel. The sound of it ripping off the roll sounded unnaturally loud in her kitchen. Still, when he wet it under the faucet and returned to clean her wounds, she couldn't take the silence.

"You called me Sexy Red."

The words were out before she could stop them, but she didn't care. She needed answers.

His hands paused on her, and she watched the top of his dark head.

"In the car," she pressed. "You called me Sexy Red."

Slowly, he looked up. Anticipation sizzled through her.

"Isn't that what I normally call you?"

Devon almost forgot to breathe. "Have we been sharing dreams?"

He braced his hands next to her hips. The move put him so close, she could see every eyelash surrounding those intense eyes. "They were real, Devon," he said softly. "*I'm* real."

Her mind went blank. She'd known it, but hearing it out loud was another thing entirely. They'd shared those dreams. They'd shared those touches, those kisses, those incredibly hot nights . . .

"But how?" she whispered. "And why aren't you more surprised? This shouldn't be possible. It shouldn't have happened."

"I'm just thanking my lucky stars that it did."

Tossing the paper towel aside, he caught her and pulled her right to the edge of the counter. Their bodies pressed tight, her breasts against his chest, his hardness between her spread legs. And yet he waited, his dark eyes staring deep.

A sound left the back of Devon's throat. He was right; she shouldn't question this. The peas slipped from her hand and clunked into the sink. She circled her arms around his neck, and her eyelids fluttered closed as his lips came down on hers.

The kiss was intense. Slow. Deep. Excitement went through her as their mouths devoured each other's. It felt so good, so right. *So real.* She threaded her fingers through his hair as his hands caressed her back.

"You scared the hell out of me today," he said, kissing his way across her cold cheek.

"I was scared, too," she confessed, "but then I blacked out and saw you."

"You saw me?"

"At a table with your brothers. I knew you'd come."

He pulled back, and a muscle at his temple flexed. "What else do you know, Sexy Red?"

Gently, he squeezed his hand between their pressed bodies. "What does 'it' have to say about us?"

Emotion filled her chest. She'd told him that in confidence, and he'd believed her. He wasn't making fun or teasing her. He believed in her abilities.

And at that moment, he had her.

Completely.

"It's the good tingle," she whispered. "The best."

That was all Cael needed to hear. He kissed her again and pulled her right off the counter into his arms. Her legs wrapped tightly around his waist, and he turned. He wanted a bed this time. A big, soft bed.

He headed to the stairs as she started tugging at his clothes. By the time he hit the second floor, he was breathing hard—and it wasn't from the exertion. He loved the feel of her hands on him. He could barely think straight as she raked them through his hair, down his back, and across his ass.

He turned into her bedroom, where it had all started. God, he needed her naked.

He set her on her feet and their clothes went fast. His hands were faster, though. He still had his pants on when he stripped her down to her lingerie.

"Damn," he hissed when her skirt slid over her hips and dropped to the floor. He stared hard at her in her black bra and panties. The woman liked sexy things—and so did he. His cock swelled so hard, he didn't know if he could walk.

Reaching out, he touched the soft lace. "I should have known." He hooked his forefinger in her bra strap and tugged her closer. "You like the feel of silk against your body."

Her green eyes flashed. "I like the feel of you even more."

It took him all of two seconds to put her on her back.

Cael had never felt a hunger like he did as he crawled over Devon on the bed. The evening was waning, but the sky was still so bright, the room practically glowed. Every time they'd made love before, the room had been cool and hazy.

Now it was hot and explicit.

And he wanted it that way. After this, there'd be no

question whether or not they'd been together. He was going to fuck her until she couldn't remember anything else.

Determinedly, he settled his weight on top of her.

"Cael," she groaned, arching her body sexily.

He laced his fingers with hers. If she said his name like that one more time, he just might lose it. He kissed her again and pressed his tongue deep into her wet mouth. Her tongue stroked back, and he felt his stiff cock jut against her belly.

"You are so beautiful," he murmured, running gentle kisses across her bruised cheek.

They'd been together before. They'd been as intimate as two people could be.

Yet this felt even better.

Touching her in corporeal form, knowing he had all of her right here . . .

He moved down to her neck. He felt the mattress shift as she started squirming underneath him. "Relax," he whispered. "We're going to take this one slow."

Her breath went ragged when he pressed his face into her cleavage. He inhaled deeply and felt her breasts press against his cheeks. Soft lace and softer woman. Reaching under her, he searched for the clasp of her bra. It gave way and the cups loosened. He nosed them out of his way.

And saw the bruises on her right breast.

Rage made his throat thick as he pushed himself up onto his elbows. "That son of a bitch."

Letting go of her hand, he lightly traced each of the five dark marks. There were three atop her plump breast, one beneath, and one deep in her cleavage. He kept his touches light, and with each soft caress, he saw the way her nipple tightened. Zeroing in on it, he swirled his finger round and round.

"Ohhh," she said. Her hands settled at the base of his spine. "Don't tease me. Not today."

He wasn't in the mood for games, either. He only wanted her to know the pleasure of his touch. Watching her closely, he let his finger and thumb close over the tight nub. Her eyelids fluttered closed, but he intensified the caress, rolling her sensitive nipple back and forth.

"Cael!" she gasped, stretching underneath him.

God, he loved hearing her say his name. Leaning down more heavily upon her, he began using his mouth. Her whole body rocked as he licked and sucked. He kept his hand working, plumping and fondling her as his mouth tugged.

"Ohhh," she groaned. "Dreamer."

Underneath him, he felt her legs part. Her body undulated and her pussy rubbed against him, begging.

He switched to her other breast.

"Ah!" She arched so hard this time she nearly lifted him.

"Slow," he insisted.

"Not this slow!"

Devon couldn't take it. Drawing her leg up for leverage, she tried to push him onto his back. "Get these pants off," she said as she struggled with his belt.

He pushed her easily back into place. "Your knees," he said firmly.

Feeling no pain, she directed her hands right back to his belt. "Please."

He stopped her by opening his big palm flat against her stomach.

"Let me love you."

Those four little words caught her attention like nothing else would. Boneless, she sagged back against the pillow. Still, her breaths went short when he caught her panties.

He settled back onto his haunches, and she looked at his face. Desire had made his cheekbones sharper, his jaw more rugged. She lifted her hips as he began to pull off the black lace, and her arousal keened when she felt warm air brush against her damp pussy.

"Sexy Red," he sighed.

Her belly fluttered when he bent down and pressed his mouth against her. He sprinkled open-mouthed kisses all over her stomach. Her muscles tightened unbearably when he stopped—right against the place where she'd told him she sensed things.

"Here?" he asked.

"There," she said tightly.

He pressed two fingers deep into her pussy, and she cried out. "Cael!"

His clothes hit the floor, and his hands settled against her inner thighs. He spread her legs wide, and directed his stiff cock at her aching core.

"Ah!" Devon gasped. The tip of his erection brushed through the tangle of auburn curls between her legs and bumped hard against her clit. Pleasure radiated deep in her womb.

"My dream girl," he said as he found her entrance.

He pushed in deep, and she twisted in delight. He felt so big and hot inside her. She'd never felt so femininely sexual in her life.

And the bright light only made it hotter. Sunshine glowed off the walls and the crisp white sheets of her bed. There was no hiding the illumination of their bodies as they came together.

"Devon," Cael groaned. He caught her hips and pulled her closer, drawing her farther onto his penetrating cock.

She drew her knees up as he began to thrust.

"You feel incredible." His fingers tangled hard in her hair as he kissed her neck.

Devon had never been so turned on in her life. She clutched at his shoulders, hanging on for dear life as he continued his torturously slow thrusts. Her butt pressed deep into the mattress with every purposeful thrust.

And it went on and on.

And on.

She gasped when he found her G-spot.

"Fuck," Cael hissed when he felt her pussy start to pulse.

His neck arched back and suddenly he was fucking her like a demon. Devon gripped him hard with everything she had—arms, legs, and pussy—as the orgasm surged through her. He let out a shout, and every muscle in his body clenched. Colors exploded on the walls around them as they came.

Finally they collapsed in a jumble. Devon flung her leg over Cael's hip to keep his long cock inside her. She wasn't ready to give him up.

She didn't know if she'd ever be ready to give him up.

For a long time, they lay together quietly. When he moved, it was to slide his hand down her thigh. "Feel okay?" he asked as he gently cupped the back of her knee.

She nodded and kissed his chest.

"It was even better, wasn't it," he said.

She knew exactly what he was talking about. As good as the sex had been between them, it had never felt like that.

"No more dream trysts." His dark eyes glowed fiercely and he drew her leg higher around his hip. "Don't come looking for me there. From now on, we make love like this."

Devon felt him swelling inside her all over again. How could she argue with logic like that? "No more dream sex," she agreed.

His hand stroked down her back, and she sighed happily. She'd much rather make love for real.

Fourteen

J ason let himself into his apartment and looked at the clock.

"Shit." He had barely enough time to pack a lunch before heading back to work. He'd gotten called in earlier to help out with that riot.

He headed to the kitchen and tossed his gym bag on the table. The world was going insane. Everyone was feeling it. If people weren't out of their heads, then they were stressed out from dealing with all the crazies.

He glanced toward the wall that separated his apartment from Tasha's. Well, maybe it wasn't all bad . . . But she wasn't crazy. She was sick.

"And stubborn," he muttered. He ran a hand

through his hair. He'd never met such a beautiful, yet frustrating woman in his life.

Why wouldn't she let him help her?

That awful feeling of helplessness rose inside him all over again, and he kicked the nearest chair. It wobbled, but tottered back into place. Apparently that workout at the gym hadn't done the trick; he was still upset about the fight they'd had.

Why couldn't she see that this was affecting him almost as much as it was her? Watching her go through this insomnia was ripping him apart. It was getting so he felt guilty about sleeping with her. He knew it helped her relax, but he was trained to treat people medically. It just wasn't in him to sit back and watch her suffer.

Turning, he yanked open the refrigerator door. A low moan stopped him cold.

Instinctively, he spun around. That had been a sound of pain.

It drifted through the wall again. That was Tasha!

He ran into the hallway. "Tasha!" he called as he knocked fiercely on her door. "Are you all right?"

A whimper wafted out of her apartment, sending dread through him.

"Tasha!" He pounded harder. "Open up, let me in."

He could hear her sounds of distress, and with each groan his anxiety increased.

Backing up, he focused on the lock. "If you're near the door, back up. I'm coming in."

Adrenaline poured through his system, and he put all his strength into the kick. Shock radiated up his leg when he connected, but the door was like the construction in the rest of the place. It gave way fast, swinging open and slamming against the interior wall.

He was inside before it bounced back.

"Tasha!" She was on the couch, rocking back and forth, hugging her stomach.

"What's wrong?" he asked as he hurried to her. "What hurts?"

"It's him; *he's* what's wrong." Her voice was low and tortured. "He's the one behind all this."

Jason looked around the room quickly. There was nobody there. "Who are you talking about?"

"Him." She pointed at the newspaper on the coffee table. "Devon conjured him," she said, her voice raspy. "I stopped sleeping when he showed up. He's evil."

Jason looked down at the newspaper. All he could see was a picture of the newspaper's new editor. She was talking nonsense. "Tasha," he said, catching her by the chin.

Her dark eyes were so pained, it hurt to look at her.

"We shouldn't have trifled. The old man told us not to trifle."

"Right," he said, pulling back to look around for clues. She was too out of it. Frantically, he looked for an empty medicine bottle or a syringe. He saw a cup of tea on the coffee table. He lifted it, and the scent hit him hard. "Ugh. What is that?"

She was rocking faster. "It all backfired. We took the utmost care, but it all went wrong."

"Tasha." He caught her by the arm and gave her a solid shake. "What's in this?"

"We used it in the potion, but we shouldn't have. It brought *him*."

Potions? Conjuring? Evil? He blocked out the words and concentrated on the things he needed to know. Her eyes weren't dilated. He caught her wrist and timed her pulse. "Is it just your stomach? Are you nauseous? Or is it a sharp pain?"

"I just want to sleep."

He hated to leave her, but he headed swiftly to the kitchen. On the counter, he saw an open jar with tea bags inside. There were only two left. He stuffed one into the front pocket of his jeans and hurried back to her.

"Come on, Whirlwind," he said as he leaned down and picked her up in his arms. He expected her to put up a fight, and it scared him when she didn't. She wrapped her arms around his neck and wearily rested her head on his shoulder.

"I'm sorry," she whispered.

The apology nearly did him in. Pushing back his fear, he hitched her higher against his chest and turned toward the door.

Mrs. Howell was just coming out of her apartment from across the hall. "Oh, my heavens. Is she okay?"

He knew Tasha would be upset with him, but he didn't have any other option.

"I'm taking her to the hospital. Watch our apartments?"

"Just go," she said, rushing him along. "Take care of our girl."

Devon woke up when the phone rang. The room was dark, but she wasn't alone. A warm weight pressed down upon her. She looked down and saw Cael's arm. Her dream man wasn't at her bedside; he was in bed with her. She smiled, but then the phone rang again.

She quickly reached to answer, glancing at the clock. She became concerned when she saw it was close to midnight. Phone calls at this hour were never good.

"Hello?" she said, looking at Cael. He slept deeply; he hadn't stirred at all.

"This is Jason Rappaport. You don't know me, but I'm a friend of Tasha's."

Devon sat up fast. "What's wrong?"

"The little whirlwind's had a bad night. I've got her at the hospital. She's mentioned you, and I thought you'd want to know."

Oh, God, the hospital? Devon slid out of Cael's slumbering embrace and gathered up her clothes. "What happened?"

"It's not serious, just a stomachache. She drank too much tea."

"The valerian?"

"You know about that?" he asked quickly. "How many tea bags were in that jar?"

"It was full."

"Shit."

Devon cringed when she heard him relay the information to somebody in the background. "Is she going to be all right? I didn't know it was dangerous."

"Normally it's not. It's a traditional herbal sleep remedy that's considered safe, but it can have adverse gastrointestinal effects." He let out a heavy sigh. "She overdid it and drank too much."

Devon eased out into the hallway. Pinching the phone between her shoulder and her ear, she started to get dressed. "She hates hospitals."

"I know, but she let them give her something to settle her stomach."

"You've got to get her out of there as soon as you can."

"I'm not going to do that," he said firmly.

Devon nearly dropped the phone. "Why not?"

"I'm taking her to the sleep clinic next."

There was no arguing with that tone of voice, and she didn't want to. She just had to get there fast. Hurrying to the window at the top of the stairs, she pulled back the shade. Her car was parked in the driveway behind Cael's.

"Tell her I'm on my way."

Devon hurried down the hospital corridors, following the signs for the sleep clinic. She hadn't been able to wake Cael, so she'd left him with a kiss and a note.

A note. God, she hated this.

She hated leaving her new lover alone in her bed. She hated that Tasha was sick. She hated the chaos that was raining down upon their lives.

Why was all this happening? *Why?*

She turned a corner, but her footsteps slowed when she saw Tasha, sitting on a waiting-room sofa with her legs curled up underneath her. Her head was resting on a man's shoulder and her arms were wrapped around his waist.

Devon hesitated, feeling like she was intruding on something private. When the handsome blond man looked up, the concern in his blue eyes reminded her of the way Cael had looked when he'd pulled her out of that crowd today.

She swallowed hard. "Tasha?"

Her friend's head turned. When she saw Devon, she went from being tired and defeated to suspicious. "What did you find out about him?" she asked, her tone scary.

"Shh," Jason said, sliding his hand soothingly down her back.

Devon moved closer. "Are you feeling better?"

"What did you learn? Did you send it back?"

Devon looked at Jason for help. He just shrugged. Concerned, she sat down. "Send what back?"

"That thing you conjured. The thing from your dreams!"

Devon's stomach dropped. She had a feeling that

had nothing to do with her premonitions, and she didn't like where it was leading. "Are you talking about Cael?"

Tasha pushed away from Jason and sat upright. Her hair swung wildly about her shoulders. "Did you find a way to reverse the spell?"

Fear sent a chill through Devon. Tasha was much worse than she'd thought. She'd taken the herbalist's words to heart, and she was obsessed to the point of fanatacism. She could see it in the tilt of her head and the glint in her eyes. Devon was glad that she hadn't been able to bring Cael with her; she could only imagine how much worse that would have made things.

"The old man was wrong, Tash." Reaching out, she put her hand on her friend's knee. "Cael's a good guy. I've spoken with him. Everything's okay."

"No," Tasha said, shaking her head fiercely. "He showed up right after the spell. That's when everything started to go wrong."

"That was just a coincidence. It's not what you're thinking."

"Yes it is. Everything goes back to him. Why can't you see that?"

"Because it's not true." Devon caught her friend's hands. "He's not some evil creature, Tasha. He's just a man."

Her friend pulled back sharply. "You're falling for him."

Devon started to shake her head but found she couldn't.

Tasha looked panic-stricken. "You slept with him! The real him. You just came from his bed!"

Devon bit her lip. Tasha had always had a nose for romance; she was able to read the interplay between men and women better than anyone Devon knew. "My bed," she softly corrected. "We've been sharing dreams, Tasha. That's what the spell did. That's all, I swear."

"Nuh uh. No!" Tasha jumped off the couch and backed away. Devon started to go after her but stopped when Jason caught her by the arm.

"Don't take it personally," he said as he watched his lover pace stiffly about the waiting room. "She's not thinking clearly right now."

Devon felt sick. "I should have paid closer attention to what was going on with her. I should have made her come down here sooner."

"We both should have," he said, regret on his face. He glanced toward the front desk. "They're overloaded with people who are having sleeping problems, but I used my connections to get her in."

Devon watched Tasha pace back and forth. Her hands were fisted as she swung them at her sides. She was inside her own little world—and it wasn't a very nice world from the look on her face.

"What's causing this?" Devon asked.

"Nobody knows." Jason rested his elbows on his knees and clenched his hands together. "There are too many people having sleep problems. The researchers are working overtime trying to find food, water, or air contaminants. There's got to be a common link, but they haven't had any luck finding it."

The desperation in his voice made Devon look at him more closely. "What do we do?" she asked softly.

His blue gaze locked with hers. "Everything we can."

He suddenly sprang to his feet, and Devon saw that a nurse had stepped into the waiting room. "Tasha St. James?" she called.

Tasha skidded to a stop. "No. I'm not going to do this. I changed my mind."

Devon and Jason both shot toward her. Jason caught her by the waist just as she turned to head to the door. "It's okay," he said into her ear. "Everything's going to be all right."

"They want to look inside my head. Don't let them. It's dark. Scary. They can't know."

Jason looked as heartsick as Devon felt. "It's okay, honey. It won't hurt," she said.

"All you have to do is lie down and sleep," Jason agreed.

"If I could sleep, I wouldn't be here!" Tasha shrieked.

"And that's exactly why you *need* to be here," Devon said. "They're just going to try to see what's happening. Don't you want to know?"

Tasha struggled in Jason's hold. He had her in a

bear hug but was muttering soft words into her ear. Devon felt tears press at her eyes. "Please, Tasha."

"What if they can't figure it out?" her friend asked, nearly hysterical. "What if I never sleep again? I'll die. It wants to kill me. I can feel it. He wants me dead."

"We have to know how to fight this, Whirlwind," Jason said. "I'll be right there with you."

"Me, too," Devon said. "You don't have to go through it alone."

Tasha's gaze snapped up. "Then do it with me."

Devon hesitated. That wasn't what she'd meant.

Tasha looked around for the nurse. "My friend dreams, and things come true. Test her, too."

Devon felt everyone looking at her. There was only one answer. "Okay, I'll do it."

For the first time in what seemed like ages, Devon couldn't get to sleep. The electrodes taped to her temples itched. The mattress was uncomfortable, and she didn't like knowing that people were watching her. She looked over at Tasha on the bed beside her. She hadn't had an easy time of it, either. It had only been when Jason had squeezed onto the twin-sized bed with her that she'd finally relaxed.

Devon's heart squeezed as she watched the two of them spooned together. This was the best guy Tasha had ever had, and from the way Jason was holding on to her, Devon knew he'd be there through the worst of it.

She rolled onto her side, and the flexible elastic belt around her chest pinched. She shifted and tried to breathe normally. She wished Cael were here for her. She was scared. Tasha's eerie sculpture had popped into her head, and she couldn't shake the feeling that her friend was slipping away to a very dark place.

What was this test going to show?

The more questions that filled her head, the fewer answers she had. This had been the longest day of her life. First, finding Cael in the office. Then fighting with that angry crowd. Finally, making love . . .

She wished so badly that she was home in bed with him right now, that none of this was happening.

"They're both out," she heard someone say softly.

She opened her eyes as the door clicked. Sitting up, she looked at Tasha, who was quiet in Jason's arms. Yes, they were both out.

It just wasn't going to happen for her; she was too agitated to stay put. She got out of bed and was confused when she didn't feel the cords tug. Looking back, she tried to see if she'd pulled something loose.

Instead, she saw herself still lying on the bed.

"Damn," she sighed. She was having another out-of-body dream.

This was not the time or the place!

Still . . .

An idea occurred to her, and she glanced toward the door consideringly. The things she saw in these dreams usually turned out to be true—like the mayor in the park. And doctors could be so tight-lipped . . .

She glanced at Tasha again. She didn't really want to leave, but Jason was right here . . .

Tiptoeing down the hallway, Devon went in search of information. It wasn't hard to find where all the doctors were. There seemed to be some kind of urgency as people in white coats streamed into a small room.

Gathering her nerve, Devon snuck in. Everyone seemed too busy to notice her. She froze when she bumped into a night nurse, but the woman looked right through her.

Everyone was staring at the screens and monitors that filled one wall. Devon stepped closer, too. She had no idea what she was looking at, other than the television screens that showed her, Tasha, and Jason sleeping on the beds.

"We've got another one," a researcher said, pointing at a printout of data. "Look at this EEG output. Large, slow delta waves. The brunette is staying in stages three and four."

"And she's not coming out of it," someone else noted. "No spindles or K-complexes are showing up."

Devon peered at the chart. She didn't know what she was reading, but she could see that Tasha's brain waves were steadily going up and down.

"There's no REM," an older doctor said, shaking his head. "How can people suddenly not be dreaming?" For a seasoned medical practitioner, he sounded upset. "I've got at least seven patients who are experiencing this—including my wife."

"Oh, my God." Devon jumped when somebody suddenly pointed at her data. "What's happening there?"

An ominous silence filled the room.

"That's the first time I've seen that," somebody whispered.

She held her breath as she looked at her screen. Her line was flat.

"There's hardly any electrical activity." The room suddenly exploded into motion. "Somebody go check if her electrodes are attached and functioning."

"She couldn't have just dropped into a coma."

A coma? Devon's head snapped toward the woman who'd made the observation. It was the nurse who'd helped her get situated for the test.

"She was perfectly healthy when she came in," the woman said, rushing to the door. "She's just doing this to help her friend."

"I'm fine," Devon called.

Nobody heard her.

Suddenly, heads bowed over the computer screens and readouts again. She glanced at the camera and saw no fewer than four people surrounding her bed.

She hurried back down the hall and found people frantically checking the vital signs of her sleeping clone.

"What's happening?"

She spun around at the sound of Cael's familiar voice.

"Oh, thank God," she said. He was here in Dreamer form.

"It's Tasha," she said shakily. "She got sick and her boyfriend brought her here. They're not paying attention to her, and she's the one who needs help—not me."

"Easy, Red. Take a deep breath." Cael looked at Tasha and a muscle along his jawline flexed. "I'm here now. Everything's going to be all right."

Devon walked to his side and gripped his hand. "It's been far too long since she's slept. It's doing things to her mind."

He went still.

"Devon," he said quietly. "Let me go to her."

"What are you doing?" she asked as he gently put her aside.

"What needs to be done." He walked up to Tasha's bedside.

"Wait," she said, taking two quick steps forward. "She's afraid of you."

His dark hair fell over his brow as he looked back at her. "Afraid of me?"

Devon squeezed her hands into fists. It was all so complicated. "She thinks that the love spell backfired, and she blames you for what's happening to her."

An indescribable look crossed his face. "She's right about that."

Devon blinked. *What had he said?*

"Don't!" she begged when he gently touched the electrode taped to Tasha's temple. "You'll wake her."

"She doesn't know I'm here, Red. Nobody does except you. Just give me a moment, and I'll explain."

Explain what? Devon hurried to his side. What did he think he could do?

"No!" She reached out and caught his arm when he brushed Tasha's hair. "The doctors are concerned about her brain-wave pattern. Don't touch anything."

"Devon," he said, his voice getting rough. "I have to."

She watched in apprehension as he reached out and settled his palm over her friend's forehead. All she could remember were Tasha's fears. She'd worried that Cael would do something to her.

"Stop," she said, reaching for his hand. "Please, stop."

"Devon," he said sharply. "Leave us be!"

Fifteen

H is harsh tone was like a slap in the face. Stunned, Devon withdrew. She looked at the way he stood over her friend, and too many things hit her at once. Betrayal, disbelief, denial . . . At the core of it all, though, was cold, bone-deep fear.

Tasha hadn't been paranoid. He meant to do no good.

Devon's protective instincts roared, and she went at Cael like a mother bear. The moment she touched his hand on Tasha's forehead, though, she went hurtling into blackness.

Dizziness filled her head and she felt like she was being pulled in a million different directions. Lights flashed and sounds hummed. She pressed her hands over her ears, but then it all stopped. She looked around frantically, trying to get her bearings. She was someplace else. Someplace dark, damp, and scary.

"Devon!"

She spun around, her hands coming up defensively. It was Tasha, and she looked like she'd been through hell. Her hair was disheveled, and her clothes were filthy. It was her eyes, though, that made Devon's fear ratchet higher. They were feral.

"We have to get out of here," her friend said. She latched down on her arm and pulled hard. "Now!"

Devon felt the threat in the air, too. Evil lurked somewhere, and it was close. Her heart began racing, and she tried to follow Tasha. But she could barely move; each step felt like she was plodding through waist-deep mud. She heard the thud of heavy footsteps behind her and the sound of snuffling. Terror rose inside her chest. She couldn't get away!

"Here! Hide here!" Tasha said, pulling her behind a tree.

Devon was breathing so hard, she knew her pursuer could hear. Yet a heavy, murky fog made it difficult to see. She felt the dew clinging to her skin—or was that cold sweat? "What's chasing us?"

"I don't know," Tasha said. Her chest was rising and falling so fast, Devon worried she was hyperventilating. "It's him. I think it's him!"

Something flapped overhead, and they both ducked. It was so hard to see.

"Which way?" Devon said. She tried to find an escape. "Which way out?"

The footsteps behind them stopped, but a low growl sounded on the opposite side of the massive oak tree. Hot, sticky breaths dampened the back of her neck.

"Run!" Tasha screamed.

Devon tried to follow, but her feet were glued in place. She turned her head and saw a massive hand coming at her. Its claws were black, and its skin was scaly. She opened her mouth to scream, but her voice was gone. All she could manage was a harsh croak as that ugly hand wrapped around her wrist.

"Devon!" Tasha screamed.

"Devon!"

This time the voice was Cael's. Devon swayed unsteadily as she suddenly found herself back in the hospital room. He was gripping her wrist, but his other hand remained on Tasha's forehead.

Devon wrenched her hand away. "What are you doing to her? Get away from her!"

"She's dreaming," he said fiercely. "You interfered and got caught up in the slipstream."

Devon's breath caught. She suddenly remembered catching him over Tasha as she'd slept on her couch. And the mayor. And her own sleeping half! She'd watched him touch her forehead that same way.

"What are you?" she demanded, the herbalist's warnings ringing in her head.

"I'm a Dream Wreaker. I—"

She didn't want to hear it. All she needed to know was that magic had begotten magic. "Stop it," she said, her voice sounding almost inhuman. "Stop whatever you're doing to her."

"No," he said, his face hard. "She needs this."

She needed to be scared? To feel hunted? To be trapped in darkness?

Rage and betrayal bubbled up until Devon couldn't contain them. This *thing* had seduced her. He hadn't really cared about her. He'd slept with her to keep her from figuring out the truth. "Get out!" she yelled.

She flung her hand toward him and red bolts flew from her fingertips. They hit him dead center in the chest. He went flying toward the wall, hit hard, and his knees buckled.

She advanced on him. "Leave us alone! Stay away from us!"

More colored lightning zapped through the air. Cael lifted his arm to defend himself, but she caught him again. He let out a pained cry and started to fade. The power kept going and chips of plaster fell from the wall. By the time they hit the floor, he'd vanished.

Devon's chest heaved. He was gone. She didn't know whether to scream or cry.

She turned toward Tasha.

"Tasha!" Anguish made it hard to talk. She shook her friend. *"Wake up!"*

. . .

Devon and Tasha sat bolt upright in bed, gasping for air, at precisely the same time. With them, an entire roomful of hospital personnel stumbled backward. Devon opened her eyes to find everyone gaping at them in surprise.

She began clawing at the electrodes taped to her skin. She wanted out of this room. Out of this place.

Tasha groaned and fell back onto the pillow. She pressed her hands to her head as if it hurt. "Oh, God. What happened?"

Devon threw a look at her as she scrambled off the bed. "Didn't you see him?"

"See what?"

"Please don't do that," a researcher said as Devon began tugging at wires. "We need this data."

"Get it from somebody else."

She ripped the pulse monitor off her finger and tossed it onto the bed.

"No, you don't understand." The night nurse put a calming hand on her shoulder. "We have to know what was happening. The two of you were experiencing very different brain-wave patterns."

As in no brain-wave pattern at all? Devon shuddered. What had he done to her all those nights?

"But then you both jumped into REM simultaneously."

She glanced up. REM—dream sleep.

"Your brain-wave patterns were identical." The older doctor seemed agitated, yet very excited. "We have to conduct further studies."

Devon's heart went out to the man, but further studies weren't going to help with anything. The problem everyone was experiencing wasn't medical. It was magical. "I'm sorry about your wife," she said. "But my friend and I have to go."

He nearly dropped his clipboard. "My wife? How do you know about my wife?"

"Tasha," Devon said, turning toward the other bed. "Come on."

"No," Tasha groaned.

"Yes!" Devon patted a hand over her stomach.

Tasha came off the bed so quickly, two of her sensors ripped right off her head. "Ow!"

"Wait," Jason said, pulling her back toward the bed. "Just a few more hours. You were *sleeping*!"

Devon's gut instinct was roaring. And "it" was wrenching. Trying not to show the doctors how much she hurt, she bent to whisper into Tasha's ear. "You were right about Cael."

Her friend's eyes rounded, and she was off the bed in a flash. Together, they disconnected the sensors and batted away doctors and nurses.

Devon looked around for a place to talk. Everyone was swarming around them and it reminded her too much of the riot. Emotion clogged her throat. Cael had rescued her then. Why had he played his role so convincingly? She'd already been hooked.

"Please," she said, pushing through the crowd of people. "We need to get dressed."

Tasha pushed her way to the front. "Out of the way, people!"

They both swiped their clothes from the top of the dresser and headed into the tiny bathroom. Devon barely made it there before doubling over and clenching her gut. Tasha slammed the door and locked it.

"What did you see?" she asked, rubbing Devon's back. "What do you feel?"

"It's not over," Devon said, pain leaking into her voice. "He's not done."

"Who's not done? Cael?"

Just hearing his name hurt. Devon looked up, her teeth clenched tight. "I saw what he's been doing to you."

Tasha's face whitened.

"I don't know how he does it or why—but you're right. That dream you had? The one where we were running from something? That was him."

"You were really there? I thought I dreamed that."

"You did. He put his hand on your forehead, and I tried to stop him. Then somehow, you and I started sharing that dream—that *nightmare*. He put it into your head. I had no idea what he's been doing to people."

Devon gasped when her stomach tightened painfully. "He's the reason why chaos is taking over. The researchers said there had to be a link."

She just couldn't believe that link was her dream man.

Tears started running down her cheeks. Even knowing what he was, she couldn't stop replaying the way they'd made love . . . the way he'd taken care of her injuries . . . the way he'd kissed her like she was something precious . . . Her heart felt as if it were ripping in two.

"That bastard," she sniffed.

"I hate him," Tasha said. "I hate him for what he did to me."

Devon dashed the tears with the back of her hand and reached for her clothes. "Come on. Get dressed."

Tasha smacked the wall with the flat of her palm. "I hate what he did to you more! We can't let him get away with it."

Devon pulled her away from the wall and began untying the knots at the back of her hospital gown. "We won't. We'll make sure he never hurts anyone again," she promised.

Tasha looked over her shoulder, her eyes narrowed. "You bet we will."

People were still waiting when they emerged from the bathroom, and every single one of them seemed to have some kind of book or research article in their hands. Devon didn't want to hear any of it. She knew what had happened, but they wouldn't find it in any of their medical textbooks.

"No," Tasha said, batting away Jason when he tried to catch her hand. "We have to stop what we started."

"What's happening?" he asked. "You can't leave. You need to be here, Tasha."

"We have to fix it," she said. "We have to stop him."

"Stop who?"

Devon could hear them talking behind her, but she just kept going.

"Excuse me. Ms. Bradshaw?"

"I'm done," she said flatly. "Find another guinea pig."

"Just one more question." The doctor stepped in front of her, and she saw that it was the one with the sick wife. "The dream," he said doggedly. "My wife hasn't had a dream in weeks. Can you tell me what yours was about? It just might give me a lead."

Devon stopped. She owed him that much. Cael had hurt so many people . . . and she'd let him.

The doctor held up a book—one that she had no desire to look at, until she saw the title. *Modern Oneiromancy*. The letters seemed to pulse as she stared at them.

"That," Devon said, pointing at the second word. "What does that mean?"

"Oneiromancy?" The doctor's bushy white eyebrows lifted. "It's the science of dream divination. Freud, in particular, believed that dreams signified—"

Freud was a hack. Cael's words rang in her head, but she tried to push them away. She didn't care what he'd said. He'd been lying to her this whole time. He'd lied about everything!

"Yes, yes," she said, making a rolling motion with her hand. "The word 'oneiromancy.' Where does it come from?"

The doctor scratched his head. "Well, that's quite interesting, if you like Greek mythology. The Oneiroi were said to be the sons of Hypnos, the god of sleep. An army of a thousand dwelled near the mouth of Hades. At night they came forth to bestow dreams of truth and dreams of lies. They were often associated with nightmares, sexual dreams—"

"A Dream Wreaker," Devon whispered. "What does 'Oneiros' mean?"

"Well, that would be the singular of Oneiroi. A dream."

A dream. Cael Oneiros. Cael Dream.

Fear pervaded her all the way down to her toes. They hadn't conjured him; they'd summoned him. Him and his brothers. She'd seen them, the Oneiroi.

She hit the doorway at a full run. She was down the hallway and in the front lobby before Tasha caught up to her.

"Let's go get him," her friend said vehemently.

"No, we have to get help," Devon said. Her stomach was aching so badly, she could hardly think.

Tasha shook her head. Her eyes were wild, just like in the nightmare. "There's no time."

Devon looked at her watch. "It isn't that long until

the sun comes up. We can go wait for the herbalist at the greenhouse."

"No!" Tasha snapped. "We have to do something now. If everything happened like you said it did, then Cael knows that you know."

Jason rounded the corner, but Devon held up a hand to keep him away. This was between her and Tasha. "He won't find me as long as I stay awake," she said, trying to find reason in an unreasonable situation.

"We can't take that chance. He's dangerous. Look at all the havoc he's caused. We have to stop him."

"I know. And the herbalist might be able to tell us how, now that we know what he is."

Tasha grabbed her and shook her hard. "I'm not going back to that freak show!"

"Well, I am!"

The two glared at each other, then Devon peeled Tasha's hands off her arms. "Stay or come with me, but I'm going now."

"Fine," Tasha said, her voice going eerily calm. She glanced back and saw Jason coming for her. When she turned back around, her face was placid. "Do what you have to do. So will I."

Sixteen

Devon sat waiting under the lone streetlight in the empty greenhouse parking lot. The building was dark; everything was quiet. She'd pounded on the door, hoping someone was still around, but nobody had answered.

Miserably, she leaned her head against the driver's side window. It could be hours until the herbalist showed up, but she had nowhere else to turn. Why hadn't she gotten the old man's name? They'd known they were in trouble.

"Trouble," she said with a disbelieving laugh. That didn't cover the half of it.

Her laugh changed into a sob, but she cut it off fast. She had to clear her head, start thinking straight.

Sniffing, she wiped her eyes. She'd never been so scared and confused in her life. What were these Oneiroi, and what were they capable of? What was *she* capable of? An uneasy feeling came over her, and she glanced at her hands.

The herbalist hadn't been lying. She was a witch. She'd seen proof of that tonight. But she didn't know how to control her powers, and they frightened her.

She'd hurt him.

Forlornly, she drew her feet up onto the seat. Knowing Cael was evil didn't make her feel any better. He'd never been evil to her. If he hadn't been hurting Tasha, she never would have been able to do what she'd done.

Devon closed her eyes. She had to toughen up. That man—*that thing*—had used her and betrayed her. Yet the battle had only begun. She had to learn from the herbalist how to get rid of him for good.

She hadn't known her heart could break any more.

Why had he done it? Why had he chosen her? Why had he just toyed with her but had hurt Tasha and the others?

Why had he made her love him?

"Cael," she whispered into the night.

Her dream man. Her nightmare.

Cael waited impatiently as Devon slipped from the hypnagogic state into the first stage of sleep. He knew he couldn't rush her, but he needed to talk to her, to explain.

She looked so pale, so frightened. He clenched his hands into fists to stop himself from reaching for her.

She was frightened of *him*.

With the things she'd seen and the way she'd gotten pulled into that dream, he could understand why. She had it all wrong, though, and there was no way he could leave things the way they were. Having her look at him with such horror had nearly killed him.

"Come on, Sexy Red," he whispered as he checked her wave patterns again. She was in stage two. He felt the rapid bursts of brain activity and the steep peaks and valleys of the K-complexes. They made his own anxiety increase.

Any time now, she could project, and he had to be ready. She'd caught him off guard at the sleep clinic. Those jolts she'd given him had clattered his teeth, but he could take a hit or two if that was what was needed. He'd do anything to get her to listen.

"Talk to me, Devon," he whispered. He waited for her green eyes to open. He always loved when that flash of recognition hit.

But her eyelids remained smooth and undisturbed. Her eyelashes fanned against her cheeks, and her breath deepened. Concerned, he put his hand over her forehead again. She was sleeping, but he didn't feel any of those unfamiliar pulses.

She wasn't projecting.

"Damn it!" Impatience hit him hard. She couldn't just sleep. Not tonight.

He had to make things right.

Settling his fingertips over her forehead, he waited for a spindle to appear. He wasn't supposed to do this, but he was on the verge of losing her—if he hadn't lost her already.

His heart squeezed, and he missed the first spindle that passed.

"Shit."

Steeling himself, he caught the second one. Determined, he started to lead her into REM. It was too early in the natural sleep progression, but he couldn't wait any longer. He wanted her on his turf, and talking to her in a dream could be the best solution of all. He could control it. She'd have to listen to him.

Thinking fast, he chose the setting. The park was nice and neutral; they'd made a connection there. He wanted to remind her of the good times. The good things.

Closing his eyes, he concentrated—and let himself fall into the slipstream.

"Devon," he said softly. They were standing next to a park bench. Their park bench. The night was dark, but the air was warm. The calm surroundings were a vivid contrast to everything he felt rumbling inside him.

She spun around. "You!" she gasped.

She looked around quickly, trying to get her bearings. When she saw the bench, she paled, and he saw her prepare to run. He caught her gently by the wrist before she could bolt.

"Please," he said. "Just let me explain."

"Explain? You think you can explain things away?" Anger and fear filled her eyes, and the park spun.

Suddenly they were in the *Sentinel*'s offices, with the sound of the presses running behind them. She was trying to change the dream.

"You can't run from me," Cael said calmly. "I'll follow until you let me tell you what you saw."

"I know what I saw!" She wrenched her wrist out of his grip, and their locale switched again.

Cael clung to his patience as they appeared in her backyard. He could do this all night long. She couldn't hide from him; he just hated that she wanted to. "Don't be afraid, Sexy Red. I won't hurt you. I could never hurt you."

"You hurt Tasha! I saw what you did. I know what you are. You're an Oneiros."

He nodded. That was precisely what he wanted to talk about. "Yes, I'm a Dream Wreaker. But I wasn't hurting her."

Devon spun around, looking for help. It was heart wrenching. All Cael wanted was to pull her into his arms. He knew that if he tried, though, he'd be in for the fight of his life. Feeling cornered, she walked backward toward her rosebushes. Every step looked like an effort.

"You've been giving Tasha nightmares," she said,

her chest rising and falling with each harsh breath. "You've been playing with everyone's minds. That's why everyone is so stressed. That's why the city is coming apart at the seams."

He held up his hands. "No, it isn't. If anything, I haven't been doling out enough dreams."

"Not enough?" Her green eyes flashed. "You monster! How can you do that to people? How can you bear to see them so scared?"

Moving toward her quickly, he caught her. She could demonize him from afar. Up close, she couldn't ignore the true him. He was the same man who'd made love to her, the man who'd given her comfort, the man who'd protected her from harm. None of that had changed.

"I'm not a monster," he said, his voice tight. "I'm just like you."

She tried to jerk away from him, and he pulled her closer. She struggled against him, trying to claw at his chest. He caught her wrists and captured them behind her back. It didn't escape his notice how her nipples raked against his chest.

"I'm just a man with special abilities."

"Those aren't special; they're evil!"

He dipped his head until their noses brushed. "People need to dream, Devon. It's the brain's way of dealing with stress. It's my job to open my charges' minds to the dream realm."

"So you can insert vile, nasty things?"

"No," he said, giving her a quick shake. "We have the ability to lead people's dreams, but it's more healing to let them choose their own."

"Tasha wouldn't choose something like that! That was a nightmare."

"And it's an important part of the balance!" Frustration ripped through him, and he looked to the stars. What could he say to make her understand?

"I am the reason Tasha has been ill," he finally confessed, "but it's not for the reason you think. Dreams are outlets. They're a safe place where people can let go of destructive thoughts and feelings like violence and anger. Without dreams, those emotions spill over into the daytime world."

The lines of her face were set, but her eyes widened. Something he'd said had gotten through.

"All the fights, the accidents, and the fires? Most of them involved my charges."

"I knew it! You did this."

He pressed her palms to his chest, right over his heart. "Tasha is sick because she *hasn't* been dreaming. Everyone is—and it's because of you."

"Me?"

"You've kept me from them," he said, hating that he had to do this to her. "You cast that spell and came into my world. I ignored my obligations and my duties to be with you, Devon. That's why everything is falling into chaos. By being together, we're tearing everyone else apart."

Devon gave a cry of denial, but she couldn't ignore what he was saying. There was a razor-sharp thread of truth in his words.

People weren't dreaming. That's what had concerned the doctors at the sleep clinic.

But she could still hear the heavy footsteps from Tasha's nightmare. She could feel those hot breaths against the back of her neck. Evil had been stalking her. "You're lying. Your brothers are here. You're all doing this; you're coming after us."

"Coming after you?" His fingers bit into her wrists. "We've always been here. We live normal lives, except at night. Instead of entering REM like other people do, we're the ones that make it happen."

"But you showed up at my work."

"Because I wanted to meet you!" he exploded.

Devon took a step backward.

"I wanted to meet you," he said more calmly. He let her go, and his hands fisted at his sides. "I've been your Dream Wreaker for the past seven months, Red. I've been standing over your bed giving you dreams, but I wanted more. So I took the job at the *Sentinel* to get closer to you. Before I got a chance to do that, though, you sat up in your bed and rocked my world."

The love spell. Devon felt her knees threaten to buckle.

"Everything changed after that."

"No," she said more to herself than him. She

turned and started to walk away fast. These things he was saying—they were too fantastical to be true.

He stayed with her, walking at her side. "You were so drop-dead gorgeous, and you wanted me. I couldn't turn you away, but the balance is delicate. You shouldn't have been there at all."

The balance. He'd kept saying that the first night she'd seen him, but she hadn't understood. She spun to walk in the other direction.

He did, too. "I tried to stop going to you, to send someone else, but you just came after me."

Because she'd wanted to see him. Devon's stomach began churning. Oh, God. She didn't want to hear any more.

He suddenly turned and pinned her against the side of the house.

"You were everything I'd ever wanted," he said bluntly. His dark eyes seemed blacker under the moonlight—and twice as intense. "You're still all I want."

Devon fought not to let her emotions overwhelm her. He was spinning everything. She couldn't fall for his lies again. "This can't be! I was just sleeping."

"You've been doing a lot more than that," he said, leaning closer. His weight brushed against hers intimately. "You've been astral projecting into the dream realm—that hazy other world where my brothers and I do our work. You were never supposed to be there."

"Astral projecting?" She pressed her hands against his shoulders. "I don't even know what that is."

He took a deep breath and sympathy softened the line of his jaw. "Your spirit travels. You know how you see your body on the bed? That's your corporeal form. You're literally splitting yourself in two—and your spirit form ended up where it never should be."

"No," she said, shaking her head. "No."

He cupped her cheek, and his fingers tangled in her hair. "You first did it in your sleep, but your powers are growing. Today you did it consciously."

"I did not! You're just trying to confuse me." She lurched against him, trying to get him off her. "I have to get rid of you. I have to send you back."

He pressed against her more heavily, and Devon bit her lip when she felt her body respond. How could she still feel for him? What was wrong with her?

"Get rid of me and evil *will* reign." He let out a breath of impatience. "Listen to me, Red. You projected today when you were caught up in that riot. I knew you needed help because you appeared in front of my bothers and me at Hooligan's."

Devon stopped. How could he know about that? She'd imagined that.

"We were sitting at a booth, and all of a sudden you were standing there. Tony nearly climbed the wall to get away from you, and even the waitress saw you."

The muscles in Devon's face went slack, and her body went numb. *What? How?*

He knew too many things. He had answers to

questions she'd had for weeks. And from the feeling in her gut, she knew he was telling the truth. About the astral projecting. About the way they'd met. About the trouble it had all caused. Horror went through her.

He wasn't the one harming everyone. She was!

"Oh, God!" she gasped. "What have I done?"

He gathered her up against his chest, and she sagged against him. All the pain and suffering, all the tragedy out there . . . She'd caused it all!

"Don't do this to yourself," he said. "You couldn't have known."

"But all those people . . . Tasha! How can we stop it?"

"You just need to let me do my work so everyone can get caught up with recuperative sleep."

Devon felt her face heat up. "So those erotic dreams we shared . . ."

"Weren't erotic dreams at all." His hands slid down her back and caught her waist. "I told you, Sexy Red, they were real. As real as you get—until tonight."

"I'm so sorry," she whispered.

"I'm not."

When she saw the arousal on his face, her body melted a little more. Even after all she'd done, after the mess she'd made, after she'd nearly blown him through a *wall*, he still wanted her.

"I don't know how I do it, though. This astral projecting thing."

"Don't worry about it. You shouldn't have to come

looking for me. I'll be in bed right beside you." He cocked his head. "If you'll still have me."

She was the one who should be begging for forgiveness.

She wrapped her arms around his neck, and his mouth came down hot and hard against hers. His tongue dipped deep and she pressed closer, rubbing her breasts against his muscled chest.

He let out a low groan. "I should have told you the truth sooner."

She nipped at his lips. "I wouldn't have believed it."

"But it might have protected you from this."

"I didn't want to be protected," she said, rocking her hips forward. "I want more than that from you."

Her mound settled right against his hard erection. He looked into her eyes, his ebony gaze burning. "I love you, Devon."

Her heart swelled. "I love you, t—"

He let out a sudden yell, and she felt the shock that reverberated through his body.

"Cael?" Every muscle in his body clenched, and fear gripped her. "What is it?"

"Ahhh!" he gasped in pain. His grip on her slackened, and he reached for his side.

"What's wrong?" She went to hold him more tightly when she felt him start to topple, only his heavy weight was becoming lighter. She clutched at him, but he went right through her fingertips.

"Cael!" Before her eyes, he started to fade. She could see less and less of him until only his eyes remained. Those beautiful, dark eyes.

"No!" she yelled as he disappeared entirely.

What was happening? Where had he gone? Was this part of the dream?

A deep pain suddenly hit her. "It" screamed, and she felt as if she were being cleaved in two. "Ahhh!" she cried.

Something was happening to him, something bad. He was hurt. She could feel his pain as if it were her own.

She opened her mouth to call for help, but nothing came out. She turned to run to her house, but her legs felt wooden. Panic seized her and her heart felt as if it were going to burst.

Where was he? She had to find him. She had to wake up!

Suddenly, she felt her body start to lift. Adrenaline pumped through her, and her fingertips tingled. She looked at them sharply. "Yes, yes!"

She needed to astral project—she needed to follow him. Closing her eyes, she concentrated hard. She pictured his deep, dark eyes. She felt his strong hands. She tasted his skin.

He'd said he loved her.

Her eyes flew open . . . and she screamed.

Cael's body was on the floor of her bedroom. He'd fallen in an uncomfortable position, and one leg was twisted up underneath him. Groaning, he writhed on the floor.

Blood was everywhere.

Devon fought hard not to get sick as she dropped to her knees. "Pressure," she told herself. "Put pressure on it."

The wound was gaping. She put her hands on it, but they went right through him. Suddenly, she realized what he'd been trying to tell her. She wasn't in his world. She could see him and hear him, but he couldn't see her. She was on another plane.

She cried out at the futility of it all. "Somebody help him!"

Suddenly, she heard a soft drip beside her. A long second passed, and it was followed by another. Fear seized her, and she looked to her left. Another pool of blood had formed. She watched, horrified, as another droplet hit. Not wanting to look, but knowing she had to, she followed its path upward.

And saw one of the knives from her cutlery block. A knife with Cael's blood.

A low moan left her throat as she saw the hand gripping it. She'd recognize that red nail polish anywhere.

Tasha's eyes were glazed, her expression vacant. Like a programmed machine, she dropped onto her knees next to Cael's supine figure.

"No!" Devon cried. "What are you doing?"

She watched in horror as her lifelong friend raised the knife again.

Bolts flew from Devon's fingertips, and Tasha bucked backward. A cry of surprise and pain left her lips. For the briefest of seconds, Devon thought she saw shock on her friend's face as she looked at Cael's body.

But she couldn't take that chance.

She channeled her emotions through her hands again, and Tasha went skidding backward across the room. She hit a chair, and it tumbled over her. Devon came to her feet, ready to defend Cael, but Tasha was lying in the fetal position.

She looked broken.

Guilt overwhelmed Devon, and she dropped back to her knees. She'd caused this. This was *her* fault. She looked back and forth between the two most important people in her life. She'd brought this upon them!

Suddenly she felt herself being pulled backward, away from the awful scene. "No!" she gasped.

She reached for Cael, for the bed, for anything she could grab hold of. Nothing caught. She went hurtling again through time and space. When she finally lurched to a stop, she was back in her car.

Alone.

"Oh, God!" Devon said, jolting upright. Disoriented, she twisted in her seat, trying to figure out what to do. The keys were in the ignition. She twisted them harshly and heard the engine fire to life. The car jerked as she put it into gear, but she slammed on the brakes.

"No," she said, her thoughts clearing. She needed help. She dug into her pocket. Her hand shook so violently, she nearly dropped her phone. Flipping it open, she hurriedly dialed 911.

"There's been a stabbing at my house," she said as soon as somebody answered, then stomped on the gas. "Send an ambulance."

Cael was dying next to her bed, and Tasha was still there with him!

"Hurry!" She gave the dispatcher her address. "Send somebody fast."

The dispatcher droned on, asking useless information like her name and phone number. Devon hung up on the woman midsentence and hit the automatic dial for Tasha's phone. She was peeling out of the parking lot when the call was answered.

"Tasha!" she said, breathing so hard her lungs hurt. "Please don't hurt him any more. Help him."

"Hurt who?"

Devon let out a cry of frustration. It was Jason. He still had her friend's phone.

"Tasha got away from me," he said, sounding as anxious as she felt. "She took my truck. What has she done?"

"You've got to get to my house," Devon said. "Fourteen Spring Road. She's stabbed Cael. She's out of her head."

"Oh, shit! Shit!"

She heard the sound of his footsteps running.

"Did you call it in?" he asked.

"Yes," she said. She took a turn on nearly two wheels. "I'm on the way, too. I just don't know if I'll get there in time."

"Let me on that ambulance," he yelled to someone. His breaths sounded harsh. "I'll meet you there."

"Hurry," she begged. "Please hurry."

Seventeen

Devon sat at Cael's bedside, watching the monitors that showed his status. She still had no idea what they all meant. She was just happy to see the blinks, the numbers, and the graphs. No straight lines anywhere. Rubbing her hands on her thighs, she looked at the IV that steadily dripped saline and medicine into his arm.

She couldn't look at the other one. It was dripping red.

Shuddering, she looked away from the machinery to the man on the hospital bed. His coloring was too pale, and he was too still. She'd hoped that he would have woken up by now. Although the doctors were playing it close to the vest, she could tell they were as concerned about his lack of response as she was.

She put her hand on his arm. All she wanted was for him to open his eyes and tell her everything was going to be okay.

"Devon?" a voice quietly called.

She glanced to the doorway and saw Jason. Like her, he was dressed in the light blue scrubs the hospital staff had loaned them. When they'd come into the emergency room, they'd been covered in so much blood. Cael's blood . . .

Light-headedness rushed over her again, and she took a deep breath. She gave Cael's arm a comforting squeeze and checked his monitors one more time, then moved to the hallway where she and Jason could talk.

"How's he doing?" he asked.

"All right, I think," she said, glancing back inside. "The doctors say he came through surgery okay. They're mainly concerned with how much blood he lost."

"Have you slept?"

"No." The best she'd been able to manage was a shower, but she still felt run-down and bedraggled.

"You should try."

He swept his thumb over the dark circles under her eyes, and their gazes caught. The look they shared was pained. Only now did they understand how important sleep was.

"I will," she promised. "You, too."

He grimaced and rubbed the back of his neck. "I guess it *is* harder said than done."

Devon swallowed hard. "How's Tasha?"

The mixture of worry and relief on his face told the story. "She's sleeping."

"Sleeping?"

"And dreaming." With a sigh, he leaned back against the wall, letting it prop him up. "The doctors gave her a sedative, and she seems to be following a normal sleep pattern."

"She's dreaming," Devon repeated. A weight lifted from her shoulders. For the first time in hours, she felt hope.

Jason rolled his head against the wall. "I'm worried about how she's going to handle it when she wakes up, though."

Devon bit her lip. "Does she realize yet what she did?"

"I don't know." His voice got heavy. "She was so out of it at the house." He glanced at her quickly. "Sorry. I know you don't want to think about that."

Devon hadn't been able to think of anything *but* that. The scene at her home had been frenzied. Paramedics and police had swarmed the place. When she and Jason had arrived, they'd found Tasha sitting on the floor, rocking back and forth.

Cael hadn't been moving at all.

Ruthlessly, she shut the memory off. She couldn't deal with it now.

"What are we going to do? Have they charged her?"

"Not yet. As far as I know, they're still at your house evaluating the scene." He glanced down the hallway to make sure nobody was listening. "You won't believe what one of Cael's brothers gave me, though."

Devon looked at him warily.

Reaching into his pocket, Jason pulled out a business card. "He's a lawyer. He told me to call him and he'd refer us to somebody for her. I don't get it. There's been a steady stream of Oneiroses coming through to see her. They don't even seem angry with her."

"Oneiroi," Devon said absently. They'd been to see Cael, too. Quite a few had donated blood, and Tony had sat beside her in the waiting room during the surgery. He'd even held her hand—after making her promise she wouldn't shock him. "I think they've had sleep problems of their own. They don't blame her."

Jason shook his head, incredulous. "His opinion was that she may have a good case for temporary insanity. Her visit to the hospital before the attack should help in her defense. The overdose of valerian shows she was unstable, and the clinic researchers can testify that she was dealing with sleep deprivation."

"And the psych ward," Devon said quietly. That was where Tasha had been taken when they'd brought her in with Cael.

Jason nodded quietly. "I'd better get back to her. Do you need anything before I go?"

Devon shook her head. "Just good thoughts."

His eyes softened, and he wrapped an arm around her shoulders. With a shuddering breath, she turned into his arms.

"It will be okay," he said as he patted her back.

"It's my fault," she said hoarsely.

"No, it's not. I keep thinking the same thing, but we can't control other people."

But she could control herself, and her actions had led to this.

"Thanks, Jason," she said with a lump in her throat. "For everything." His quick actions had saved Cael's life.

He gave her a tight hug and kissed the top of her head. "If you need me, you know where I'll be."

Devon put on a brave face. "Go. Tasha needs you."

He glanced to the hospital room behind them. "And your guy needs you, too." Stuffing his hands into his pockets, he headed down the hallway.

Inside Cael's room, Devon's gaze went straight to the monitors—no change. She sat close to the bed and caught his hand.

"Come on, Cael. Come back to me." Nothing would be okay until she saw those dark eyes.

Still, he didn't stir.

She'd run out of tears a long time ago. Now every time she wanted to cry, her eyes felt gritty and heavy. Still holding Cael's hand, Devon rested her forearm on the bed next to his hip and tiredly lowered her head.

She had nothing left in the tank. Worry and stress had drained the last bit of energy from her. She'd kept going on heart alone.

Exhaustion overcame her, and she went into a slumber so deep, her body became heavy and her thoughts stopped entirely. She was at peace for a long, long time . . .

Until she felt a presence.

Devon's heart jumped. Slowly, she lifted her head.

Deep, dark eyes stared back at her.

Her breath caught. "You're watching me again, Dreamer."

He materialized at the bedside. "Right now, that seems to be about all I can do."

Holding his side, he walked to the window and gingerly leaned against the sill.

Devon wanted to jump up and run to him, but something wasn't quite right. She glanced to the bed. For once, she wasn't the only one splitting herself in two. And he looked as pale and unmoving as he had for the past three hours. She pushed back her fear and stood. Carefully, she walked over to the window. "How are you feeling?" she asked.

"Good enough to have you come closer."

"Are you sure?" She glanced to the bed. "Should you really be projecting like this?"

"Get over here."

She let out a heavy breath and sat next to him. He

still felt as big and warm as always. Yet when he lifted his arm to put it around her, he groaned.

"Stop," she said, worry wringing her insides. "Don't hurt yourself any more than you already are."

"I'm fine, Devon," he said grumpily. "You're not. I can see it."

It was true, she wasn't. Taking care not to disturb the bandage at his waist, she slid her arm around his back. He felt so good. So warm. *Alive.* She rested her head on his shoulder. "I'm so sorry."

His finger flicked away a stray tear that ran down her face. "None of that. We talked about this."

"But that was before . . ." She looked at him apprehensively. "Do you know what happened?"

His expression turned grim. "I've been watching over Tasha."

"You're in no shape to help her."

He gave her a comforting squeeze. "I'm not, my brothers are taking turns. They're lined up over her, in fact. I guess it doesn't hurt that she's cute."

"What about the rest of your charges?"

"Reinforcements have been called in." He looked chastened and wearily rubbed his whisker-roughened face. "They should have been called in long before now."

Devon hated that he was hurting—and in so many ways. She carefully wrapped both arms around him, wanting to make everything better. She looked across the room and got all choked up when she saw the two of them sleeping together, him on the hospital bed and her at his side.

"Why aren't you waking up?" If she held on to him tightly enough, could she pull him back to Earth with her? "The doctors said you should be awake by now."

"Don't worry. I recuperate better this way." He ran his hand up and down her back but winced when it pulled his stitches.

Devon quickly relieved the vise grip she had on him. "Just tell me you're getting better."

"I will," he said through clenched teeth.

She clutched her hands anxiously in her lap. "What can I do to help?"

His ebony eyes flared as he looked into her face. "Still love me?"

Her breath caught. The last time she'd said those words to him, they'd been terribly interrupted. "Always."

He pulled her closer and his lips brushed across hers, heartbreakingly sweet. When his tongue darted out, though, it got a little spicy. Devon gasped when his arms came around her. This time she felt the strength that underlay his weak appearance. He was healing— and healing fast.

Her hands fluttered about his shoulders. "We shouldn't do this."

"Why not?"

"Because I shouldn't be here . . . in the dream realm."

He reluctantly pulled back. "That *is* what got us into trouble in the first place."

"Get better, and we can be together," she said. "I'm waiting for you."

His dark eyes turned serious. "You know you can't come for me here anymore. I love you, Sexy Red, but if this is going to work, you have to let my spirit fly."

"I know," Devon said. "I will."

"I'm not a normal man," he warned.

"And I'm not a normal woman." She cupped his face and looked into those midnight eyes that she'd fallen in love with so long ago. "But if I can only have part of you, I'll take the real man over the dream man any day."

Epilogue

The Solstice Arts Gallery was busy with activity when Devon stepped through the front door. The lobby was bright compared to the dark evening outside, and it felt warm and comfortable after the chill in the fall air. Patrons walked to and fro, some taking hors d'oeuvres off the plates of passing waiters, but most looking at the paintings and sculptures set up around the spacious room.

Devon's breath caught. "Oh, Cael. Look!"

The door closed behind him and he stopped by her side, just as surprised as she was.

Tasha was having her fall showing, and it looked to be a huge success. Devon couldn't contain her relief. She and Cael had expected a large turnout for the show, but they were somewhat fearful for the quality of the crowd. There were bound to be gawkers. There were still curious types out there who would show up just to see how her friend was coping after her breakdown.

Instead of hiding it, though, Tasha was putting herself out there for the world to see. The exhibit she'd put up was bold and unapologetic. Unflinchingly truthful. She was admitting to the difficulties she'd faced getting to this point in her life.

"So what do you think?" came a quiet voice from their left.

"Tasha!" Devon said, turning. Holding her camera aside, she gave her friend a hug. "It looks fantastic."

"Gutsy," Cael agreed.

Tasha bit her lip. "Are you okay with it? I should have told you, but I just got so busy trying to get everything ready . . ."

He walked to her and dropped a gentle kiss on her forehead. "I'm fine with it. You know I had some responsibility in things, too."

"Me, too," Devon whispered.

"Hey, buddy, watch those lips."

Devon looked up to see Jason headed their way. He looked drop-dead handsome in his dark suit and blue tie. With his sandy blond hair, he looked like a business mogul who took afternoons off to surf. She threw him a wink. "You clean up nice."

He grinned back at her and handed her a drink. "So do you."

Devon felt Cael's possessive gaze run over her. She was wearing a tailored jade green dress that would have looked very elegant if it weren't for the plunging neckline, which gave it a daring edge. She knew he liked it, he'd already peeled it off of her once. That's why they were late.

Jason held out a beer. "I didn't think you were the white wine type."

"Thanks," Cael said appreciatively.

Devon let her own gaze do a little traveling. If anyone looked good in formal wear, it was her Dreamer. He hadn't been the only one stripping a lover.

Tasha came closer, her silver skirt swishing with each step. "You're working?" she asked.

Devon glanced down at her Canon EOS. "We thought the *Sentinel* would give you some positive coverage to balance out the critics." She glanced around. "Looks like you don't need it."

Tasha smiled. "You can't ever have too many good reviews, although yours might be biased."

Together, they looked around at all the activity. The Gallery was packed, and from the sold tags going up on the pieces, it looked as if serious buyers were in the house.

Assuming the role of hostess, Tasha held out her hands presenting her work. "Which side do you want to see first?"

Taking a bold move that none of them had expected, she'd divided her showing into two distinct parts:

Before and After. On the left side of the room were the sketches and pieces she'd done before her breakdown. The colors were dark, the subjects darker. It was an unusual turn for her, strictly outside her known repertoire. Yet something in the pieces called to people, as if they knew the feelings being represented but had never been brave enough to admit to them. The Before side was packed.

"Let's go to the After," Jason said.

Together, they moved to the brighter, sunnier portion of the exhibit. Cael's arm slipped around Devon's waist, and she lifted her camera for a quick shot of Tasha and Jason smiling at each other.

The After side was positively exuberant. Bright colors and detailed work showed Tasha's recovery. Devon recognized one drawing she'd even worked on while still in the hospital. Sleep, counseling, and dreaming had brought her friend back.

Tasha turned, a cautious but hopeful expression on her face. "I have something I want to give the two of you." She looked specifically at Cael. "I know I can never tell you how sorry I am, but I thought this might show you."

Reaching out, he quickly caught her by the chin. "You know I don't want your apologies. I just want your happiness."

She grinned at him. "I think you'll like it."

He smiled back. "Then show us."

Tasha led them to the center of the room, where

Before met After. There in the spotlight stood a piece that joined the two together.

"Oh, Tasha," Devon said, letting her camera drop around her neck.

"Amazing, isn't it?" Jason said quietly.

Devon moved closer to Cael, and his fingers tightened against her waist.

The central piece in Tasha's display was the sculpture that had consumed her during her downward spiral—only now it was accompanied by a mirroring shape. The dark, howling form had been done in brass; the bright, serene figure was fashioned from silver. The two specters curled around each other as if in a delicate dance.

Moving closer, Tasha stroked her hand down the silver form. "It's about the balance that needs to be kept between darkness and light."

"Sadness and happiness," Jason said.

"Fear and passion," Devon added.

"Nightmares and dreams," Cael finished.

Tasha looked at him steadily, happiness shining in her eyes. "I knew you'd get it. I call it *The Oneiroi*."